There's No Place Like ...

Tessa McWatt

MACMILLAN CARIBBEAN WRITERS

MACMILLAN
CARIBBEAN

For Sean, Alanna, Kiera and Charles

Macmillan Education
Between Towns Road, Oxford, OX4 3PP
A division of Macmillan Publishers Limited
Companies and representatives throughout the world

www.macmillan-caribbean.com

ISBN 0 333 94615 4

First published 2004

Typeset by StoreyBooks
Cover illustration by Gina Foster

A catalogue record for this book is available from the British Library.

Printed and bound in Thailand

2008 2007 2006 2005 2004
10 9 8 7 6 5 4 3 2 1

Series Preface

There's No Place Like ... is a remarkable reinterpretation of Frank Baum's classic children's story, *The Wizard of Oz*. Tessa McWatt's Dorothy is Beatrice, a rebellious Guyanese eighteen-year-old of rainbow ancestry, whose yellow brick road in the form of an airline ticket carries her all around a world of wonders in the discovery of essential home truths. Her travelling companions, each on his own quest for courage, love or wisdom, are three unusual youths from Ireland, China and India. Other favourite *Oz* characters have also been ingeniously updated, perhaps the most original being the wicked witch, who takes the form of a paranoid young career woman dangerously obsessed with marketing experimental genetically modified foods.

The Macmillan Caribbean Writers Series (MCW) is an exciting new collection of fine Caribbean writing which treats the broad range of the Caribbean experience. As well as novels and short stories the series includes poetry anthologies and collections of plays particularly suitable for arts and drama festivals. There are also works of non-fiction such as an eye-witness account of life under the volatile Soufriere volcano, and another of the removal of an entire village to make way for an American base in World War II.

The series introduces unknown work by newly discovered writers, and in addition showcases new writing and favourite classics by established authors such as Michael Anthony, Jan Carew, Ian McDonald, G C H Thomas and Anthony C Winkler. Writers on the list come from around the region, including Guyana, Trinidad, Tobago, Barbados, St Vincent, Bequia, Grenada, St Lucia, Dominica, Montserrat, Antigua, the Bahamas, Jamaica and Belize.

MCW was launched in 2003 at the Caribbean's premier literary event, the Calabash Festival in Jamaica. Macmillan Caribbean is also proud to be associated with the work of the Cropper Foundation in Trinidad, developing the talents of the region's most promising emerging writers, many of whom are contributors to MCW.

Judy Stone
Series Editor
Macmillan Caribbean Writers

Macmillan Caribbean Writers Series

edited by Judy Stone

Novels:

> *Jeremiah, Devil of the Woods:* Martina Altmann
> *Butler, Till the Final Bell:* Michael Anthony
> *Such as I have:* Garfield Ellis
> *The Boy from Willow Bend:* Joanne C Hillhouse
> *Dancing Nude in the Moonlight:* Joanne C Hillhouse
> *Ginger Lily:* Margaret Knight
> *Exclusion Zone:* Graeme Knott
> *The Humming-Bird Tree:* Ian McDonald
> *There's No Place Like ...:* Tessa McWatt
> *Ruler in Hiroona:* G C H Thomas

Plays:

> *Champions of the Gayelle:* (ed. Judy Stone)
> *Good morning, Miss Millie:* Alwin Bully
> *Duelling Voices:* Zeno Constance
> *The Rapist:* Pat Cumper
> *More Champions of the Gayelle:* (ed. Judy Stone)
> *Dog:* Dennis Scott
> *You can Lead a Horse to Water:* Winston Saunders
> *One of our Sons is Missing:* Godfrey Sealy

Stories:

> *Going Home, and other tales from Guyana:* Deryck M Bernard
> *The Sisters, and Manco's Stories:* Jan Carew
> *The Annihilation of Fish and other stories:* Anthony C Winkler

Georgetown, Guyana

"It's not fair, I tell ya, not fair at all," her brother whined, shaking his head and pushing his chair back from the kitchen table. He stood up and skulked out of the kitchen, skirting into his room at the end of the salmon-coloured corridor, slamming the door. Beatrice looked up from her breakfast, guiltily. Her eyes darted first towards her mother, then her father. Her mother stood up with a sigh and cleared the lunch dishes. Her father caught Beatrice's eye and gave her a quick wink, reassuring her that it would all be fine.

"I can't help it, can I? I didn't ask for it, and, besides, he's the one people give all'a everything to, even when he makes trouble or plays the fool," Beatrice said.

She wanted to say more, or to run after Felix and offer to share the money – little brothers had to be indulged or they turned against you – but she could feel she wasn't going to need Felix's allegiance soon. She was sensing freedom like a window opened up in a stifling room. Her mother did the washing up, while her father turned his attention back to the document on the kitchen table.

The day was growing hotter, and outside a kiskadee repeated its singing question over and over from its perch in the five-finger shrub in the back garden. Kiskadee! Kiskadee! It was like a holler for attention. Beatrice fell under its spell. Her thoughts floated out through the window and into the garden, where she imagined she sat perched next to the bird, considering the world from its perspective. *"Qu'est-ce qu'il dit?"* That was what people said the bird's call signified in language. A bird that would call throughout the day: "What's he saying? What's he saying?" She mouthed the bird's song back to it as she gazed at the white stripe over its eye. From the shrub, she thought, the whole world would seem poised within a kaleidoscope. Everything like a series of reflections in loose glass spinning and rotating to form what, uniquely, Beatrice saw as reality. Her image of the world was shifting and complex, changing shape with the slightest turn of perspective.

Mid-afternoon, and the neighbourhood was peaceful and quiet, but in the distance Indian music and radio programmes streamed softly through the air. The bird hushed. Beatrice's thoughts floated up even higher, and drifted to way above the confident concrete houses of this neighbourhood known as Kitty. Children played in the swampy gutter making their toys whiz over the grass. Mini-buses soared by in the main street, honking, stopping at the corner, music blaring out of the doors as they slid open to let in their next customers. Mosquitoes hovered, waiting for the sun to drop before they would descend and torture the neighbourhood with their bites and buzzing.

The voice of her mother called her down from her dreamy perch in the sky and back into the kitchen.

"Felix knows you were Mavis's favourite," she said to Beatrice as she wiped plates with a dishtowel. She turned to her husband and added, "Maybe we could buy him that new bicycle, what you think?" Beatrice's father merely nodded, concentrating on the legal document in his hand.

Beatrice focussed her attention back onto the issue of the inheritance. She was trying to be cool about the news, but inside she was erupting like a happy volcano. The pattern was typical for her family. Felix was hot-headed and showed it, erupting easily and visibly at the slightest provocation, but she held back, sometimes hiding her joy, often her anger – her feelings bottled and capped like a fizzy drink. But now… Ten Thousand Dollars! And US money, not hopeless Guyana dollars. A car, clothes, make-up, a DVD machine for all her favourite movies – these possibilities flashed through her mind as she tried to look serious in front of her parents.

She caught sight of her reflection in the china cabinet glass. The thrill showed itself in the tapered, almond-shaped corners of her eyes. A delighted glimmer shone there. Adjusting her fringe, she pursed her lips. She was special after all. Perhaps other people would take her fantasies more seriously now. After years of feeling odd, an outsider even among her closest friends, Beatrice had stopped trying to cap her imagination, and she privately revelled in it, dwelling in a mental landscape where everything was possible. She stared into the china cabinet and drifted off. Behind the glass, a small porcelain statue of an English gentleman tipped his top hat, congratulatory. She smiled back and winked.

Since the age of twelve, Beatrice had accepted the different world that existed independently in her mind. The world of her parents didn't make much sense, with its practicalities, its restrictions on time and place, and rules upon rules, which she often just forgot to follow. She felt most comfortable in her imagination. Her best friend, Stephanie, would sometimes have to wake her from deep reveries, and Beatrice would feel cheated out of magic, with a feeling like being in a cinema when the projector suddenly flickers to a halt. She loved to escape to the movies. The more fantastical the better, the more special effects the keener she was.

And she wanted to act.

Acting had been her vocation since primary school when she would play schoolyard games and take centre stage. She was "brown girl in the ring...tra la la la la..." twirling her curly hair and bouncing up her skinny bottom, so convincingly that it almost looked womanly. It was a talent her Auntie Mavis had also recognised. But there were things even Auntie Mavis didn't know about Beatrice. She didn't know where her mind would escape to when it seemed she was daydreaming. She didn't know the secret cinematographic powers that allowed Beatrice to see things no one else was seeing, like the hibiscus flowers which swayed as though they were dancing too, or the guinep trees that began to shimmy to the tra la la magic of a song.

Beatrice liked action movies and flashy love stories, while Stephanie preferred classic films from the 1940s. Stephanie told Beatrice she was like a movie star from the past: "You have lips like that old-time star, Judy Garland, and, girl you're enough like her and she dreamin' self. As if somebody really did snatch you up and tek away your soul while you standin' right in front of me," she complained.

Now, at the kitchen table, Beatrice pictured Judy's sultry lips and big innocent eyes. She ran her tongue over her own lips. Any actress worth her salt needed to make the most of her lips, she thought. And now she was going to be able to buy the new make-up she'd seen at the cosmetics party Stephanie's mother had given. The colours from New York were wild – purple and shades of pink she'd never dreamed of – and she had her eye on one of the orangey-brown tones. With that colour on her lips she could easily fit the part of Cleopatra. She imagined the sound of the Nile lapping at the bow of her riverboat. Antony's head was nestled in her lap.

The front door slammed.

Beatrice was jolted back into that other reality of the kitchen. Her mother sat down at the table next to her father and examined the document. The afternoon humidity swirled in when Felix stormed out, probably headed to see his friends and to console himself with sweets because Auntie Mavis had not left him any money.

Beatrice's aunt had been sick in the hospital for months, calling her family to her bedside, telling them her life story. She had always wanted to leave Guyana, to travel the world, but she hadn't been able to because she had been obliged to look after her parents as they got older. After they died, she never found the courage to travel by herself.

In hospital Auntie Mavis seemed different. Her carefree spirit had sunk down into a cavern of regret. But she was still full of wisdom. Not married, but never without a boyfriend as a young woman, Mavis had been the talk of the town. Charming by half, she would attend cricket matches and horse races wearing outrageous outfits of chiffon and silk, with feathered hats and boas. She opened a shop in Stabroek Market with the last of the money from her father's business, and there she sold rare books and paintings. She also did palm and tarot-card readings. Beatrice gained a deep respect for the occult under Auntie Mavis's tutelage. And it was in that bookshop that art first made its claim on her. Books and images were one thing, but she would also watch Auntie Mavis paint as she sat by the seawall and interpreted in watercolour images a collection of fantasy figures emerging from the sea. Confused in the beginning, Beatrice soon began to see shapes there too, detecting wave after wave of possible adventure approaching the shore like an armada of movie images. Sometimes her aunt's paintings brought her to tears.

Now Auntie Mavis was gone, died of a stroke in her sleep, and Beatrice missed her with an ache in the mornings. Her aunt had been the only person who came close to understanding her, especially since she had turned eighteen and was approaching adulthood. Now there was no one to talk to. Just Felix, who at fourteen was a growing annoyance in Beatrice's life. Felix was sentimental and a bit touchy. Beatrice couldn't help but tease him. The restrictions on her inner life, in the context of her family and surroundings, sometimes made her feel she would burst. And in those moments, she often took it out on her little brother.

But her aunt had left Beatrice money, and now everything was going to be fine. Beatrice's mind raced to the carpark at Joe's Motors and she saw, could almost touch, the one she wanted. A sporty new Ford. She would be able to escape Felix and his silly friends by driving away from them, watching the dust flying up in their faces from the wheels of her shiny new...

"There's a condition," Beatrice's mother said, bursting into the fantasy. She looked up from the document with a sly smile forming. Beatrice felt her hopes suddenly snag in the "this-will-be-good-for-you" ropes of her unfanciful parents. She looked back at the porcelain gentleman in the china cabinet. He rolled his eyes at her and then held his hand over his mouth in a wide, exaggerated yawn.

"The condition has to do with how you spend the money. Mavis thinks your attitude to life is missing something important, and right as rain she is. She's been clever by adding this last bit. Here," her mother said as she handed the document to her husband, "see what you think."
Beatrice's father carefully read the passage she pointed out. His face was serious-looking, the fleshy folds around his mouth and chin drooping like the skin on an elephant. When he'd finished reading, the same sly smile that had appeared on her mother's lips a few minutes previously also slid onto his.

"Perfect," he said and put the letter on the table. "But you sure she's ready for this? She's never done this kind of thing before, and mostly we see her around here poutin' and stchupsin' at everything. This requires huge responsibility," he said looking at Beatrice.

"*Kiskadee! Kiskadee!*" the bird hollered from its perch. Her father's look and the bird's call made Beatrice nervous. What were they talking about?

"I know," her mother said, "but this is the way she'll learn it."

Beatrice became uncomfortable. What were the smug looks on their faces? She glanced back at the china cabinet. The porcelain gentleman was still and statued again. She caught her reflection in the glass. Her face looked confused, her emotions escaping even though she tried to hide them. What an odd face, she thought. She was an unusual mix-up of all of Guyana's people. Her looks were unique in the town, at school, with her friends, and even within her own family. Was this why she felt bottled up all the time, too many people living inside her? Maybe with Auntie Mavis's money she'd be able to buy the fashionable clothes and make-up her mother had refused her in the past. Her imagination jump cut to Kirpalani's, where she was testing out blush and eyeliner, lipstick and mascara...

"Beatrice will get the money only if, before she settles into any life, either an academic one or a working one," her father said ominously, looking first at his wife and then at Beatrice, "she uses the money to finance a trip around the world."

CUT! The imaginary scene at Kirpalani's dissolved, and Beatrice sat, awestruck, at the kitchen table as her mother and father stared at her, waiting for her response. Wow. That was a shock. Resentment began to surface. What about her freedom? Her car? Her new clothes? Could Auntie Mavis have forgotten that Beatrice told her she wanted to act on the big screen? Mavis had wanted her to attend art school in England or Paris, but Beatrice argued that her destiny was as an actress, not a painter. Movies were all that mattered to her.

"ACTION!" a director's voice in her imagination called out. In the next scene she was inside the china cabinet with the porcelain gentleman:

> MAN: *My good lady, I sense your distress.*
> BEATRICE: *You sense well. They seek to torment me.*
> MAN: *Come away with me, my lovely...*
> BEATRICE: *Come away? But where?*
> MAN: *Where? Hollywood, of course...*

BEATRICE: (gasps)
MAN: (smiling as he kisses her hand) *Where else do statues talk?*

That was it! She could use Auntie Mavis's money to get her to Hollywood where she'd be discovered. Auntie Mavis would have wanted that for her. Hollywood is the only place to be, every actress knows that. In Hollywood all you have to do is work at a restaurant for a few months then be discovered. That's how it happened for another girl who had fled Georgetown and was given a part in a studio picture. And that's how stardom had come for many great actresses.

Beatrice winked at the porcelain gentleman, brushed back her fringe with her hand and was about to get up from the table with a happy bounce.

"There's one more minor condition," her father said, stopping Beatrice as she was about to tell them what her first port of call would be. She settled back in her seat. "The only place you can't go on the trip is to California. If you go to California the money will be revoked and put towards your university education."

"CUT! CUT! CUT!" the voice in her head shouted. Sabotaged. Beatrice felt the wavy surge of betrayal in her guts. Why would her aunt have done such a cruel thing?

"But…" Beatrice started to say, but gave up, feeling defeated. She tried to imagine a scene in which she had a passionate argument with her parents, telling them she would not do what anyone else wanted her to do. Then she'd turn on her heels and head out of the front door and walk towards her waiting limousine.

But in reality she was stranded. How could her aunt have been so cruel as to keep Beatrice away from the one thing that would make her happy? What was she supposed to do now? To wander around the world for months like a hobo? Beatrice slouched in her chair. Once again, reality was bearing down on her.

"And she wants you to be adventurous in your choices – India, Africa, the Far East," her father continued, looking a little worried. "Bea, it sounds like quite a challenge," he said finally, then looked anxiously at his wife. "I don't think I like the idea of her going by herself. It's not safe." He put the document down on the table.

Beatrice picked it up to examine it. Surely there was something in the fine print that got her off the hook and allowed her to get to California or to forget this ridiculous idea altogether and to buy a car. At the very bottom of the document was a paragraph in Auntie Mavis's own hand that said:

> And Beatrice is to understand that something will come to her along the journey. A kind of treasure that she has no way of imagining at this moment but which, I assure her, will make itself known by the time she has done as I asked. By the end of the trip she will know what I mean.

Her aunt was a mystery. The bottled-up fizzy parts of Beatrice began to stir. She felt excited. But what if nothing came of it? What if her aunt was wrong and all that life offered was this daily feeling of being out of place and restless? She put the document down.

"We know lots of people, Nathan, we can make sure she's looked after," said her mother. "My sister is in Miami, my cousin in London, you have family in Canada. She won't be alone, and, if you ask me, it's time she took responsibility for herself," she added firmly.

Beatrice glared up from the table to cut her eyes at her mother, who wiped down the counter and sink with a sponge.

"But Africa?" her father said. "There's so much instability there, tribal wars and what not…"

"Well, it doesn't say she must go there. You're right, we'll have to so some research, make sure the places she goes are safe," her mother answered.

Later that evening when Felix was already in bed, Beatrice approached the sitting room where she heard her parents deep in discussion. She stood outside the room a few seconds to listen.

"She hasn't seen a single project through to the end by herself. All she does is make up stories and play the fool. I don't know how this will be any different." Her father's voice sounded tired and slightly sad. Beatrice felt a lump grow in her throat.

"But like this, she'll have to fend for herself, and she'll start to appreciate what everyone around here has always done for her," her mother said.

"But I don't think she really wants to go. Maybe she should just get a job and then decide if she wants to go to university. She's got the brains, we know that."

"She doesn't apply herself. Always off dreamin' and watchin' movies. She's been sitting around mooning about far off things since she finished school. That girl doesn't know what's important in life."

A mosquito buzzed near Beatrice's ear and lit on her neck. She swatted it, crushing it with her fingers. Then she hit her head, then her shoulder, then her own backside. Really playing the fool and pretending to punish herself for what her parents thought of her. You silly child, she whispered, as she tapped her head once more. But the lump rose higher in her throat, and she swallowed hard so as not to cry. Was this really true about her? She'd heard it before. It was how her teacher from Bishop's High School had characterised her too.

Ms Buckley used to pick on Beatrice for daydreaming in class. She called Beatrice naïve and lazy when she'd present reports based on movie versions of books instead of the books themselves.

"Movies are shallow forms of entertainment, Beatrice," Ms Buckley would say in her most stiff, phoney British accent. But then her accent would falter when she continued, "It's like goat bite you, and you're off in a dream."

Beatrice would hold her tongue and feel the lid tighten on her emotions. She wanted to holler out that movies had the power to change the world. She knew that Ms Buckley would not agree. That baiara-faced woman only knew to talk about business and advancement.

"This country has to concentrate on business and technology," she said many times a day, and Beatrice would watch the underbite of the woman's two protruding bottom teeth pointing towards her nostrils, and she'd have trouble not giggling. Baiara-fish Buckley, Stephanie used to call her. Only Stephanie and Auntie Mavis really understood how Beatrice felt about movies and art.

"Girl, you don't listen to any nonsense from baiara-face. I tell you, you are a star. A star is born. That Judy Garland was just like you." Coming from Stephanie, who was the coolest girl at Bishop's, this was a real compliment for Beatrice. Stephanie's mother was poor and supported herself and her daughter by having home cosmetics parties. They got a small sum each month from Stephanie's father, who had deserted them several years before. He now lived in Berbice with a new woman, and he rarely ever saw his daughter. But Stephanie was doted on by her mother. With the little money left over after groceries, Stephanie's mother dressed her in stylish clothes. Stephanie wore her hair in dozens of thin plaits, and her wide face and jet-black eyes were wildly decorated. Her mother made sure they had a good television, and friends from Miami had bought them a DVD player. That meant Stephanie could rent the old movies she loved. Together she and Beatrice first watched *It's a Wonderful Life* and *To Kill a Mocking Bird*. Under Stephanie's influence, Beatrice was slowly becoming a film buff. Lights! Camera! Action!

But her parents didn't understand how it felt to be eighteen and stuck in Georgetown. Her father had chosen to return after many years of living abroad in Canada. He and her mother ran a successful restaurant in town. Not wealthy, unable to afford luxuries, they nevertheless had saved for Beatrice's and Felix's education, and had put all their hopes into their futures. Studying, chores, and marathon telephone conversations with Stephanie composed the dull rhythm of Beatrice's days. On weekends she would visit Auntie Mavis or attend dances at St George's Hall with her friends.

She liked the dances, where she could feel the drums right in her bones. She was a wild dancer, jumping-up to the latest calypsos, or grooving to Hip-Hop and Garage Jam. She also liked the acid jazz that came from London and the salsa from Miami and California. The film in her head would become an MTV video and she'd imagine herself leaping across a stage, twirling and falling to the floor in the splits. Then CUT! PRINT IT! Next she'd be driving down the long, filmic stretch of highway along the California coast in a Malibu convertible.

She would usually sit out the slow songs. They were too predictable, and she knew dancing slowly with a man was just a way for him to get hold of her buttocks and feel them up. And the boys at school were immature. She preferred the company of her friends, and to jump-up at parties in groups. Most of her friends had already had sex with boys at school and elsewhere, but Beatrice had never had a serious boyfriend. She had been waiting for a chance to meet someone special... perhaps in Hollywood.

She tuned back into her parents' conversation.

"If only she'd come back down to earth," her mother lamented. Beatrice's hurt feelings turned to anger and she burst into the sitting room, surprising her parents.

"I'm more on earth than you can ever imagine, Mommy. And there's more to it than this old-time town, so I've made up my mind to go on Auntie's world trip. And you can't stop me from going where I want." She had no idea that she'd made up her mind until that very moment. The pronouncement made her feel powerful, full, and for the first time she felt like she was standing up to her parents. "I'll pick the places I want to go, not you, and I'll go for as long as six months, but if I don't want to be away for the whole time, I can come back whenever I want."

"Of course you can, Bea. You come back whenever you want. We don't want you to be away so long anyway," her father said, a little teary.

"But you must promise to stay with your relatives. Family is what will keep you safe, Bea, and you'll need to feel protected when you're so far away," her mother added.

Beatrice had always thought of her mother as courageous, always doing things on her own, travelling to Trinidad and Jamaica for supplies to use in the restaurant. Safe was never a word she had associated with her, but her comment made Beatrice wonder if she was really so brave after all.

"I want to go where I don't know anyone. I want to know what it's like to be a complete stranger somewhere for once," she said to them firmly. One of her problems with her life in Georgetown was that everyone always knew her business, what she was doing, where she was going, and who she was with. She thought of Auntie Mavis, who had always wanted to see the world, to walk as a stranger through city streets, to be romanced by foreign, mysterious men.

"You don't have to be totally alone," her mother said, "we'll plan it all out from here and set up an itinerary for you, to make sure you can get in touch with people or that we can get in touch with you, somehow, wherever you are. There's always email, and we'll give you a phone card."

Beatrice smiled. Her spirits were lifted. Life looked promising after all. If she couldn't go to Hollywood right away at least she would get away from Georgetown and be on an adventure to find people who would understand her.

July 23

Dear Diary

I haven't done this since I was twelve, but here goes. I used to think diaries were for girls, but I guess if I'm going to be alone I'm going to have to talk to someone. The scene is this:

WIDE SHOT: On the road near an old stone farmhouse in a former Soviet country, a semi-attractive, hypersensitive, and over-analytical young woman is sitting by a stone wall, her feet aching from all the walking she's been doing. She takes a journal out of her rucksack and begins to write: "Help! I'm going mad with silence. No one to talk to." She writes and writes in the journal. Cars pass her, their passengers looking amused and yet keeping their distance.

Man, I hope I don't go too crazy!
I'm headed to Miami first, to make Mom happy, and I'll stay with her sister and family. My cousin, Johnny, is sixteen. I haven't seen him since he was toddler. I hope he's cool..
After Miami, I head to Mexico, which was my pick. Mom really didn't want me to go there, but my motives are really about California. If I'm in the neighbourhood, I might, by chance, meet someone from Hollywood. Mexico also has good beaches. Dad insists that I visit his relatives in Canada, so want to take in the sun while I can. Then it's Europe.
My knowledge of Europe is simple, school-bookish, and probably misshapen by World War II movies. My image of it is jumbled like the debris in a bombed building. In school you learn a lot about war:

bombings, rations, RAF pilots and nowhere to find stockings or buy sweets. And Auntie Mavis's stories embellished this view. The only time she was away from Guyana was during WWII, when she went to England to work with the West Indian regiment. When I think of England I think of little pies, little houses, and old castles. I wonder what it's really like.

Mom has left the rest of the destinations up to me. I have an open ticket, can stop anywhere I like after London, as long as I keep going in one direction and return within six months.

Part of me still can't believe this is all happening. Yesterday I ran into my biology teacher, Ms Buckley, in Stabroek Market. With a very snarly tone in her voice, and that innuendo of "you're just a good-for-nothing," she asked me what I was getting up to. When I told her about my trip she seemed surprised.

"Well, well, well... I never thought you'd be interested in anything so sophisticated my dear... you never seemed..." and then she paused, as if trying to avoid the insult that was frothing up on her tongue, "... well, let's put it this way, you never seemed anything but a dreamer."

I held my breath and felt my blood boil. That crab-ass baiara-face has never said a kind thing to me, and she vexed me fa so. She is always going on about what this country needs: "This country needs big business, technology, and genetic engineering to improve agriculture," she said many times. And she believes that if we could clone animals we'd be able to make better breeds to improve the food supply and to make the people in this country rich. "You see any corporations bringing their work here? We need corporations, we need capital," she would say to us during our biology classes. "Once this country was a world leader in bauxite. We could do it with something else, we just need the capital." I think she's confusing "capital" with "inspiration," and the woman frightens me with her narrow-minded views. Buckley and I are totally at odds in our way of seeing the world.

One day in class, when I had tolerated just enough of her talk, I blurted out, "But we could do with some culture too," and she stopped in mid-sentence and glared at me. She's never forgiven me for that. It's not that I disagree that we need technology, it's just that people need all kinds of ways of being fed. Stories, paintings, and beautiful things around them. Imagine! Everything's possible.

She barely passed me in that course. But now I won't have to fear running into her for at least six months. I can't wait to go.

Outside the airport departure gate, Beatrice swallowed anxiously, but the lump in her throat was rising; she held back tears. Standing in front of a sweets vendor, she decided to buy five packages of tamarind balls, worried she was not going to taste her favourite sweets for a long time.

"You sweet 'nuff," the man said to her as he handed her the change. She looked up at the man and in a film-cut second he shrank to become the porcelain gentleman in her china cabinet.

"What are you doing here?" she asked, astonished.

"I could ask the same question," he answered in his stiff, nineteenth-century accent.

"I'm leaving," Beatrice said.

"Good for you. And remember, follow the road of your heart," and then he bowed to her. She shook her head quickly to clear it. The sweets vendor was still staring at her. He gave her a wink. Beatrice rushed back to the gate, her family and friends.

When her mother approached to kiss her, Beatrice pretended she had something in her eye, so that her mother wouldn't notice she was crying. Beatrice's lips and cheek were trembling. Suddenly she wanted to be a little girl again, but she knew she'd have to be strong, for her mother's sake. "Ya have to show a brave face," her mother would always say whenever Beatrice faced a new challenge. Beatrice put her arms around her mother's shoulders and held on tight.

"You're a big baba after all," Felix teased.

"And you're too much botheration," she shot back, but added a smile, as she released her mother's shoulders.

Her father gave her an affectionate bear hug, and Beatrice could see that his eyes were glassy with tears, his nose red. His top lip quivered slightly when he spoke.

"Now, remember, if you ever need anything, or if you're ever in a difficult situation, you call, immediately, night or day." He hugged her again and then held her shoulders at his arms' length to look at her. "You be good to yourself, you hear me?"

"Yes, Dad."

Beatrice looked at Felix, who was still putting on an air of being jilted by Auntie Mavis. She reached to touch his shoulder, but Stephanie moved between them and threw her arms around Beatrice as her own tears streamed down. Stephanie held a tiny present wrapped in glittering pink and gold paper, tied with pink ribbon.

"So ya not going to forget me when you're going about with all those fancy new people you'll meet," Stephanie whispered as she placed the gift in her friend's hand. She released Beatrice from her hug.

"Open it."

"Ya, open it," said Felix, curiously.

Her family watched as she opened Stephanie's gift – a locket on a chain. Opening the locket, Beatrice saw a photo of herself, Stephanie and four other girls from Bishop's High School on the seawall, all waving as if to a boat far out on the sea. Each girl was smiling, looking happy to be either welcoming a coming ship or bidding farewell to a departing one.

She wanted to cry again, but she resisted. To buy this locket Stephanie must have spent her entire allowance from her mother's make-up parties. Beatrice put the chain around her neck, and the locket rested on her chest. A feeling rose up within her like the swelling sounds of the first few bars of music.

She tapped Felix on the arm gently and grabbed him to hug her. Then she turned away abruptly as the tears fell. With one final wave and blown kiss, she entered the departure lounge of the airport.

She listened to the announcements, waiting eagerly for her flight. When it was finally called and she was in the plane, the rush of excitement overwhelmed her. This was it. She was heading off, and there was no turning back. The excitement felt like that first moment in the cinema, as the lights go down, the music comes up, and the opening credits appear on the screen. In the rush of speed as the plane sped down the runway, she let go of her doubts. As it tipped up its nose to leap into the sky, Beatrice felt her stomach lurch towards her chest. She was totally on her own, with no one to help her, no one to talk to except her diary. And who was she doing this for? For Auntie Mavis? Mavis never did anything without a clear purpose or keen understanding. Where was Mavis leading her? The music to accompany life's new movie grew louder and more melodic. Beatrice began to hum.

Miami, Florida

August 2

Dear Diary

Touching down on the tarmac in the US of A was exhilarating. America was once referred to as the land of the free, home of the brave, but once when Daddy was asked by someone at home if he wanted to emigrate there, he answered, "not a chance, na ah, not me, man," and I've always wondered why. Everything happens here, that much I do know. Miami looks busy, but there's the beach and the gentle palms, and I can't wait to find out what else.

As the plane lifted off and left Cheddi Jagan Airport, I watched my country disappear, all that muddy brown water of the Demerara River flowing out to the sea. I had mixed emotions, like the muddy water itself. Will I miss it? Good-bye Georgetown, good-bye mosquitoes, good-bye all the hard-ass teachers at Bishop's, especially the horrible Ms Buckley. Good-bye to everyone who never understood me and what I wanted to do. I'll get to Hollywood yet.

August 4

Dear Diary

Miami hit me like a stray bullet. Nothing like the movies. Not what I expected at all. It's crammed full of buildings, tall gleaming towers and shorter, white and pink walk-up apartments over shops with glaring neon signs. And more cars than I've ever seen before. Mom's sister and her husband have a small apartment on Rainbow Road in Dade County. Here there is certainly nothing that I would have recognised from the screen, except perhaps in one of the gangsta rap videos Felix watches obsessively. Swarms of different gangs roam the area, and all the gang boys have their own cars. Even my young cousin, Johnny, has a car of his own: an old, fire-engine red, souped-up Ford Blazer with fat tyres and double exhaust. He buffs and shines it while he hangs out in the street in front of the apartment building. His friends pull up and the whole bad lot of them stand about talking and smoking, just liming. The music is loud, loud, and most of it's in Spanish. Some of it I recognise from MTV.

A few of the girls have their own cars, and the music blaring from them is mostly Hip-Hop. As their cars pass by the front window, I create girl-band videos in my head with these girls on stage leaping and twirling, tummies exposed, hips gyrating. Spin, slap, steady, one, two, three, and a big finish, arms in the air. I like the Spanish songs best, but I don't understand their lyrics. Johnny's friends are mostly Cubans. He doesn't speak Spanish, so it's a mystery to me how he feels he belongs among them. Johnny's background is almost as mixed up as mine. He's part Amerindian, African and Indian. But he dances like a Latino, gels his hair, and plasters it to his head to look like his padres. I think that's how he fits in here. Funny to see him looking like he belongs here, when he could be in Georgetown looking like he belongs there. A change of hairdo and clothing, and … presto! … new roots, new blood. Could I ever belong here?

Johnny and his friends are part of the blaring Miami night. He says he'll take me out with them tomorrow, so I'm excited.

Tonight we went to a fireworks display at a downtown park. Auntie June had told me that Miami puts on fireworks like nowhere else in the world. She was right. It was truly amazing, as though the sky was exploding and opening up to let me through. I have a feeling that's what the rest of my trip is going to be like!

WWW.WORLDMAIL.COM

Mom and Dad

> I'm writing this from an Internet café in Miami, sipping my
> mocha Java supreme. The living here is fine fa so! I arrived
> safely at Auntie June's, and the family has been taking good
> care of me. Their apartment is smaller than I thought it would
> be. Not everything in America is big. In the last few days I've
> started to feel America under my skin. Miami is a mix-up,

> like me. This neighbourhood has many people from the
> Caribbean, especially Jamaicans, Cubans and Dominicans. But
> they talk as though they've just popped out of the same
> American movie. They love movies here, that's for sure.
> But, while walking in the street, I have wondered if the whole
> neighbourhood won't eventually explode in a Hollywood shoot-
> up ending.

> Auntie June took me to fireworks that would have stopped
> your breath. I've never seen anything like that in Guyana. She
> is very generous, and she keeps telling me stories of you,
> Mom, when you were girls in Guyana. Seems you liked to
> imitate people's walks. Maybe that's where I get my thirst
> for acting in the first place.

> Johnny is a fancy pants, oddy, if you ask me. He feels
> pressured to do whatever his friends ask him to do. Friendly,
> like Felix, Johnny seems so grown-up, even though he's only
> two years older than that bratty brother of mine (just pulling
> your leg, bro. Tell Felix I say hi). Johnny is taking me out
> tonight. My week here will go by quickly, I'm sure. Got to run
> now. It takes me so long to type that I've used up my half-
> hour already!

> Lots of Love, Bea

Beatrice's face was close to the mirror, one finger pulling tight the skin around the bottom of her eye, the other hand delicately dabbing eyeliner near the eye's tapered corner. Suddenly there was banging on the door, startling her, causing her hand to jolt, the charcoal eyeliner smearing a thick black line from her eye to her cheek.

"Come on, girl, get movin'," Johnny shouted from the other side of the door.

"You told me seven o'clock!" she yelled back.

"Ya, mi padres are here, get a move on."

It was like a stage call: knock, knock! "You're on in five minutes, Ms Douglas."

She cleaned off the charcoal smudge and quickly brushed her eyelashes with mascara. She combed down her fringe, picked up her purse and headed to the elevator with Johnny.

In the street the Latin beat was contagious and Beatrice moved towards the waiting cars as though she were dancing. Three boys wearing jeans, singlets and red bandannas tied around their foreheads stared at her from their comfortable poses, leaning on one of the souped-up cars.

"Eh, *cómo esta, hermana...*"

Beatrice didn't understand, but knew the boy was flirting with her.

"Hey, she's my cousin, careful," said Johnny to his friend. "Like a sister, so off limits."

But the handsome, manly-looking boy ignored his warning and walked towards Beatrice.

"*Mi muhere*, what is your name?" the boy asked. He was tall, tanned and muscular in his singlet. His brown hair set off his dazzling green eyes.

"Beatrice," she said timidly, looking towards her feet.

"Ah, Beatrice, like a goddess, I think, no? Was there not a goddess named Beatrice? And me, I am Dante."

Beatrice didn't understand what he was getting at. She kept her eyes on the ground. If only Stephanie could see her now, what would she think? This boy was probably her age, but he seemed much surer of himself than the boys at home did.

The gang piled into two cars. Beatrice sat in the back seat of Johnny's Blazer, squeezed between a younger boy and a girl named Con. "Constanza," Johnny said carefully to Beatrice, to make sure she got it right. "She's Puerto Rican, and barely speaks English yet. She's a friend of Dante's." Dante was driving the convertible just ahead of them, and Beatrice felt a pang of longing for him. She wanted to see those eyes again.

They drove slowly through the Miami evening, down the streets in the East End, and the night seemed to rumble with sound and sensation. The car turned up Ocean Boulevard, and along the strip of road that hugged the beach music blared from almost every car, as though in competition to be the loudest. The sounds mingled and the rumble became a tinny blare. Beatrice's mind wandered. Her imagination took her to a love scene, by the ocean. On the beach Dante was running towards her as she ran towards him. They embraced and fell to the sand, the sea washing up around their entwined legs...

"Hey, you want to get some fries?" The voice was Johnny's, startling her out of her reverie. They had arrived in the parking lot of McDonald's, and the rest of Johnny's friends were already out of the car and in the restaurant.

"No, I'm not hungry, thanks," she said, a bit dazed. She got out of the car and leaned against it looking up at the Miami night sky. The moon was nowhere in sight, the stars barely visible because of the city's lights. When the others came back outside, they stood about, chatting, telling jokes. The Spanish flew by her, as she understood only the occasional word. She grew restless. What was she doing here? All dressed up and hanging out in a parking lot?

Finally Dante approached her.

"Now, *hermana*, you are Johnny's cousin, but you look different from him. What are you?"

What are you? What was that supposed to mean? Beatrice was silent for a few moments.

"I'm Guyanese," she said, matter-of-factly.

"Yea, but I mean, you look like you could be Chinese, or Black, or even Latina, like us, or a bunch of different things. Not like the other girls in our hood, is what I mean. And not like Johnny."

Beatrice was put off slightly. What was he trying to say?

"Is that a bad thing?" she asked, looking into his eyes.

"Oh, no, no, no, my beauty ..." and he approached her and held the back of her head and pulled it towards him. He kissed her straight on the lips. A movie kiss. But her eyes were wide open; she was shocked by the passion coming from him. Her heart started to race. Along with the homeboy talk, the kiss was the only other thing in Miami that was like the movies. She gulped and pulled back, her body tingling and confused.

"Yea, and these lips. This neck ... I like these," he continued, and kissed her neck and shoulders. He stopped and looked at her seriously. "But baby, if the others catch me with you I'm doomed. I mean we have rules in this gang. And if they catch me with someone who looks like she could be from another hood, maybe one we're fightin' with at the moment, I could lose face."

"CUT, CUT, CUT!" the director's voice blared. Lose face? What was she hearing? Beatrice was stunned. Was Dante telling her that he couldn't be seen with her because she didn't have the right background? She had thought America was the one place on earth where people mixed freely. What was going on?

She picked up her purse from the ground where it had fallen, and marched over to Johnny who was sucking on a straw, sipping a milkshake by a car with the younger boys. She knew he had watched Dante kiss her.

"Look, Johnny, I gone. Take me back to the apartment."

"What? We just got here? What's wrong with you, anyway?"

What was wrong with her, she wondered. Why couldn't she fit in?

"Nothing, fed up with this nonsense. You're meant to be looking after me and I want to go back."

The two of them got into Johnny's Blazer and pulled out of the parking lot. Through the window of the passenger seat Beatrice watched Dante strut up to the young Puerto Rican girl, Constanza, and take her hand to his lips to kiss it. She felt her stomach turn with distaste and jealousy. She slumped in her seat and kept her eyes to the front all the way back to Rainbow Road.

Mexico City, Mexico

Dear Stephanie,
Nothing is as we thought it would be.

Miami is like a hall of mirrors. Everything you think is familiar seems to bend out of shape and come back upon itself to make for confusion. I don't have a donkey's clue what's going on there. Did you get the postcard I sent describing that two-mouthed Dante, talking sweet to me then saying nasty things about me to his friends? To be honest, I wanted him to fancy me, but when I heard that ridiculous gang talk coming out of his cocky-boy mouth, it turned me off. He reminds me of Jason, from our 5th form, so full of himself. And besides, his eyes weren't that special — I think he was wearing tinted contact lenses.

Mexico, now that's a city.

It's a beautiful city when you look closely. But on first appearance it's huge and stink. It's so high up in the hills that I can hardly breathe by the end of the day when I return to the student hostel. Mommy would get a fright if she could imagine me here on my own in such a big city and staying in this hostel.

The city's buildings are old, like at home, but older, made beautifully out of stone, and not crumbling down like the ones in Georgetown. In a museum at the city's centre, murals by a Mexican painter named Diego Rivera line the length of the gallery's walls. Breathtaking, with blood and passion. Men dying for passion the way they do in the movies. That's the kind of man I want, fa sure! I know you think I'm always going on, but I'm sure one of the men in the paintings had the exact same face as our teacher Mr Martinez. And while I was standing staring at it an English-speaking woman came up behind me and said, "Yes, I think you're right," and then just walked away! I don't know if she was reading my mind or talking to someone else, but it fright' me some. Then again, I'm finding everything a surprise. Maybe all of life is a movie in itself.

I'm propelled on a journey taking me to things I would never have thought I'd be interested in, like museums and churches. Of course, to enter a church you needn't pay anything, so they have become a refuge and a resting spot for me, where I can go, sit, and be alone without being afraid. I do a lot of thinking. I often get an inkling of what it is I'm supposed to be looking for (my heart's desire? a career? a better education?), but I remain simply fascinated by the people I'm seeing. Mexico is amazing. Parts of it are modern and European, and other parts are just shambles.

As you know, Mexico is the original capital of the great Aztec Empire. The sprawling ruins around the city are impressive. Old, old stone with symbolic carvings of sun gods and fertility goddesses. I knew nothing about the Aztecs before I came here, and now when I look into the faces of some of the people, mostly the poor who live in the shacks on the outskirts of the city, I can see the faces of those Aztecs. And reflected in those faces are more faces, like the ones of the Amerindians in the interior of Guyana. And some of them even look like Felix. Some days I feel like I am in a carnival or circus, with halls of mirrors, tricks and shows going on around me. But I realise that perhaps I'm being shown a giant collage of one big human family. Yesterday when I was sitting in a café drinking my first tequila (it tastes a bit like paiwari),

a few people came up to me and spoke in
Spanish, asking for directions, thinking that
I must be Mexican too. I guess I do sort of
look like them, except for all this curly hair.

Well, Steph, I'm off to see the grand square,
to sit near the fountain with the statue of a
woman holding an arrow as though she's about
to spear the world and make it hers. I like the
look of her, and spearing the world's just what
I intend to do.

Hope all is well with you back home. I hope
Raj is treating you well and not just using
you. I'm convinced you should dump him and wait
for passion, girl!

Love,
Beatrice

Knowing she shouldn't be anywhere near California, Beatrice
felt a guilty tingle in her spine as the coach pulled into the
station in Tijuana. The temptation had been too much for her.
So close to California and yet so far? She had to come to see if
she could feel California just across the border. Would there be
Hollywood scouts in the area, looking for someone just like her?
Would she dare take the three-hour bus ride up the coast that
would take her over the border into San Diego?

The ride to Tijuana had been an air-conditioning nightmare,
with the system going on and off, malfunctioning for the entire
journey as the coach wound its way slowly through dry town
after dry town. Beatrice stared out the window at the array of
donkeys and their riders, groups of barefoot children playing
with sticks and wheels, and women selling fruit by the side of
the road. Along brown roads through a landscape of baking
desert, they finally arrived in the city that had a reputation for
being the toughest town in Mexico.

The air was hot but breezy when she got down from the bus
and made her way out of the terminal. Tumbleweed drifted by
her and dust blew up into her eyes so that she had to shield
them. She walked through the dry, Wild West streets with her

backpack feeling heavy. She stopped in front of a colourfully painted and ornate church and decided to enter it to escape the persistent sun.

"*Psst… psst…*" she heard over her shoulder as she sat in the back pew. Beatrice turned around to see a boy about her brother's age, with a wide face just like Felix's, beckoning her.

"I show you something," he said with a thick accent, and continued to wave her towards him. Beatrice looked around to make sure the boy was talking to her and not someone else, but she was the only other person in the building, so she took up her backpack and followed him to a door at the back of the church. He led her outside into a deserted courtyard. She stopped, suddenly frightened of where he was leading her, but he turned and beckoned her again.

"Come, you will like this, you will want to take me to California…"

Merely the mention of the place of her dreams made her follow the boy through the courtyard to a small row of shacks and caravans.

He walked into a rickety caravan and held the door open for her. Beatrice hesitated but stepped inside. She was shocked by the glitzy décor of red, yellow and green banners with the faces of Hollywood movie stars on them. Mirrors of all shapes and sizes hung on the walls, along with a variety of hats and ornate masks. More shocking was the presence of about a dozen cages containing lizards of all sizes. Beatrice's skin crawled at the sight of the prehistoric-looking creatures champing on bits of lettuce or carrots.

"Here, this one, this one is special," said the boy, his face even wider now in the excitement of sharing his treasures. He opened the largest cage and took out a rabbit-sized iguana. Beatrice felt dizzy. The boy took a tiny top hat down from the wall and placed it on the iguana's head. He pressed the play button on a boombox on the counter. The tape started to play a rock n' roll tune that Beatrice was familiar with but couldn't name. Her mind drifted for a few seconds as she tried to recognise the tune, but suddenly the iguana had risen up to rest its front legs on a large stone in its cage and was standing on its hind legs. It started to move to the music like Elvis doing the twist. The boy grinned and turned the volume up. Beatrice's eyes widened, her jaw dropped. She blinked and shook her head, convinced it was another of her fanciful movie visions, but this time the scene didn't cut out. The iguana still gyrated to the music.

"You give him a job in a movie?" the boy hollered, over the loud music. Beatrice realised he thought she was from Hollywood. She was speechless. "Umm... Umm..." she muttered. She was confounded. Is this what awaited her in the world of movies? "Sorry, I have to go," she mumbled and walked quickly out of the caravan and back through the church courtyard. She kept up her swift pace through the archway to the street, then down to the busy main road and the coach terminal. It was time to get far away from Tijuana. A weirder scene than her imagination could produce was enough of a warning that she should not tempt her luck and go against her aunt's wishes. California was too close. She bought a ticket back to Mexico City, where she'd be able to use her airline ticket to take her somewhere else.

GREETINGS FROM TIJUANA

Dear Felix, The photograph on this postcard is of a cockfight in the Wild West, but take my word for it, there are more than just roosters on show here in Tijuana. If I told you, you wouldn't believe me and might take me for mad. They call Tijuana "wildest of the wild," and so far they're not fibbing. Mexicans look like you, and that's why I'm sending you this card. Have a look at the boy with the hat. I met a boy your age who really reminded me of you. I don't know if I'm cut out to be part of the world circus, but I've barely used my ticket, so I suppose there's no turning back now. Be good to Mom and Dad.

Love, Bea

London, England

It was the middle of the night somewhere in the black sky above the heaving Atlantic Ocean, on British Airways Flight 92 from Toronto Pearson Airport to London Heathrow. There was no turning back now, but Beatrice had considered giving up and going home several times in the last week.

After leaving Mexico, she flew to Toronto to stay with her uncle for a few days. Toronto was another place that wasn't as she expected. It was big and clean but crowded, with lots of people from every country on the map, many of them from the Caribbean. As she walked through the ordered downtown streets, she saw people she almost recognised, because they looked like people at home. The bewildering range of shops and restaurants included those selling produce from all over the world; she bought a curry and roti from a take-away in the West End. She became homesick and disoriented. With something exotic to eat on every corner, Toronto was like a great stew of people of all different nationalities.

Her uncle's very young wife was a Chinese-Canadian, and for dinner on her first night at their home Beatrice was served a wonderful feast of Chinese food. She was shown how to make dumplings, and encouraged to visit China on her trip:

"In China," her uncle's wife said, "every day is magical. Ordinary things do not happen in China. All is extraordinary. Toronto is something, very good for making a living, but China... now that is a very special place."

Beatrice liked her new aunt very much. She was tuned in, like Auntie Mavis, but this aunt had seen the world, and she convinced Beatrice that there was much to discover and that she had to continue her journey. So, here she was on an overnight flight to London.

The fantastical in-flight movie, about the quirky woman who discovers food portals on the Internet that will download chocolate, was now over. The credits were rolling. Beatrice took off her headset and rubbed her tired eyes. Along with the other passengers who were still awake, she was trying to get comfortable, with the hope of sleeping before the early morning landing in London. She squirmed in her window seat, unable to find the right position. She was edgy and sleepless. The tall man beside her, who was travelling to London to visit his sister, whom he hadn't seen in twenty years, was snoring. Beatrice looked at his knees. His long legs protruded into the space in front of her, making her even more uncomfortable.

The flight attendant with sparkling green eyes walked up the aisle and stopped at Beatrice's row.

"Trouble sleeping?" she whispered over the snoring man in the aisle seat.

"Ya, I can't seem to get comfortable…" answered Beatrice.

"I'll be back in a second," the flight attendant said.

She's beautiful, thought Beatrice. The woman had the kindest face and smile Beatrice had ever seen. Beatrice wondered how many times she had travelled across the Atlantic and how curious life would be always flying back and forth through time zones and over oceans. Wouldn't she feel lost? How would she ever know what was real or when was when and where was where?

"Here, drink this; it will help you relax," said the flight attendant when she returned. She handed Beatrice a steaming cup of broth.

"What is it?" asked Beatrice, intrigued, yet instantly trusting the gentle soul of this woman who seemed sent from heaven.

"Just a little concoction I made up myself… with special plants and herbs that I've collected from around the world. Mostly from Africa. You have a big adventure ahead of you; you need to rest," she said then slipped away down the aisle.

How did she know that? thought Beatrice. Beatrice had not spoken to the flight attendant other than to say hello upon boarding and then "chicken," when offered a choice of meals. But from the moment she boarded the plane she felt at ease with the beautiful auburn-haired woman with feline eyes the colour of emeralds.

Beatrice sipped the broth. It warmed and soothed her. She could feel herself relaxing. She slid up the shutter to look out of the window. Blackness everywhere. Suddenly something billowy and white flew by. A sheet? A flapping, falling piece of heaven? She slid the shutter closed. The plane bumped in an air pocket and dropped suddenly. Then it started to shake. Turbulence. A few more seconds and the turbulence got worse. The plane bounced through pockets of air, up and down, up and down. The overhead compartments rattled. The seatbelt light blinked and came on with a ping. The sound of seatbelts being fastened clicked throughout the cabin.

Beatrice slid open the shutter again. More debris flew past the window. The objects took on strange shapes with their speed. Nervously, she took another sip of the slopping broth, then a deep breath to stop the panic from rising. The man next to her began to stir; his snoring stopped with a snort on one of the deep drops the aeroplane was now repeatedly performing. A bell pinged overhead. The captain's voice was serene as it came over the loudspeaker:

"Ladies and gentlemen, we are experiencing a bit of turbulence related to a summer storm over the Atlantic. In the interest of your safety, please buckle your seat belts and stay seated until the seat belt sign has been switched off."

Beatrice adjusted her seat belt, clicking the clasp open then closing it again. She touched her forehead. She had started to perspire. The turbulence made her queasy. She wondered if she should have stayed on the other side of the Atlantic. She gulped back the remaining broth, feeling for the first time vulnerable to the power of weather. The aeroplane was being tossed around in the sky.

Suddenly... flash!

The wing of the plane was illuminated in the lightning that struck just above it. Beatrice gasped. The man beside her groaned. The turbulence got rougher. The overhead compartment above her fell open and a large blunt case fell from it, striking her on the head. Instantly unconscious, she felt nothing further in the realm of the senses. She did not hear the cries of the other passengers, nor the "Help! Help!" of the man beside her. Her mind swirled up to the ethers where she saw visions of houses on clouds, of landscapes blown up from the earth, of shimmers of lightning like fireflies in an open field.

Inside the cabin the rhythmic light show startled the other passengers, and their gasps seemed contagious. The air outside the window seemed to be swirling, as though on the edge of a huge tornado. While the lightning kept up its strobe light effects, the woman behind Beatrice started to pray.

Blackness swirled into Beatrice's visions. She didn't hear the voice of the flight attendant and the others trying to help her. The blackness carried more strange shapes. People, monkeys, lions, dragons, then automobiles, palm trees and a large, snapping lobster. Suddenly the shape of a giant fish zoomed by as if it swam through the air or flew like a Barbados flying fish. Then the plane dropped sharply through the air. There were loud cries from the passengers, some screaming, and many breaking into tears. Beatrice could almost detect the sounds through her unconscious haze, but she remained far away. More shapes flew into her vision: a billowy figure of a woman with the wind in her long hair drew up beside the plane. The ugly woman, showing bared, spiky teeth, was laughing at Beatrice. She shook her fist at her in anger. Beatrice let out a scream, comforting the flight attendant, who realised that Beatrice was not so deeply unconscious.

"Hello, hello, come back to us," said the soft voice into Beatrice's ear. Slowly Beatrice regained consciousness. When she opened her eyes she was staring into the emerald eyes of the flight attendant.

"We lost you for a while, but I think you're going to be fine. Here..." And the flight attendant held a cool damp cloth to Beatrice's forehead. "And drink more of this," she said, offering another cup of broth.

While Beatrice slowly caught up to time and reality, the bumpy ride continued. The sound and smell of passengers using their vomit bags made her feel sick herself. She closed her eyes again and tried to imagine a happy movie, not a disaster movie. She searched her childhood memories for a comforting image and conjured up Julie Andrews on a bed singing *My Favourite Things*.

The captain's voice was less serene the second time it came over the loudspeaker:

"Ladies and gentlemen, the storm we're experiencing is quite severe, and we expect to be feeling its effects for the rest of our time in the air, so it's imperative that you remain in your seats and keep your seat belts fastened until further notice."

No one was asleep any more, and the tension in the cabin was high. Beatrice continued to sing in her head. She tried to ignore the feeling of being tossed around in the open and black sky.

August 25

Dear Diary

BRUDUM! The pounding on my head before I blacked out had a horrific sound. And the sound of the plane landing on the tarmac was a BRUDUM and BADAM as though we'd plunged from the sky to hit the earth. What a flight. A nightmare, truly a nightmare. "Ghastly"… that's a word they use a lot in England. Ghastly, ghastly, ghastly, as they say in those old-fashioned films I watched with Stephanie. They say "ghastly" a lot for the weather, the actors groaning "ghastly, ghastly" as they come in from the cold and rain, rubbing their hands together for warmth. Well, the flight was more than ghastly. It was wretched.

The only consolation was the kind and beautiful flight attendant, Linda, the most gorgeous woman I've ever met, with beauty that emanates from within. The special broth she gave me was comforting, and she pampered me after I came to. I have what feels like a cricket ball growing out of my head where the suitcase hit me. Linda says I should go to a hospital to have it checked out, but I dread hospitals.

When we arrived at the airport I could hardly see straight. With the bump, the airsickness, and the jetlag, my body felt like it had left me in the night. Before I got off the plane Linda gave me a small clear sweet to suck on, which helped to clear my head somewhat, but I have remained in a slight fog ever since. She wished me a great trip and said, "Be sure to see Africa," which shocked me, because I still have no idea how she knew I was on a world trip!

Dozy, and waiting for my backpack to arrive on the carousel, I decided I needed a trolley, so took one from the line of trolleys at the far end of the terminal. Pushing it back to the carousel I marvelled at the foreignness of London, the small details in people's clothing, and, of course, their accents. I caught sight of an advertisement for the Tower of London, and just then, I ran into a very rude woman. Literally, I ran into her with my trolley by accident. I was shocked speechless, and the woman took this as a statement of intent. "Watch the hell where you're going you stupid little tourist. Don't you know how to push a cart?" she said in a loud voice, rubbing her ankle. "This is Europe. Handle it," she concluded and turned up her hooked nose at me. Before I could blurt out an apology, she had turned her back and was walking away. I caught up with her and called out: "Sorry about that," thinking she'd turn and we'd patch things up. But she raised her hand in the air in a brush-off to me and I was stopped in my tracks. Her accent was American, so I don't know what she was going on about Europe for in such an uppity tone. She was a shortish woman with wildly curly red hair and fair skin. My hair bristled at her rudeness, and I wanted to tell her to go to the devil, but I held my tongue. I was happy to get away from her.

I barely remember the drive to my cousin's house in Notting Hill. He picked me up at the airport, and no wonder he had trouble recognising me, I was probably the colour of ash. The trip through London was all a blur.

But here, now, as I sit out on the balcony of my cousin Eddie's flat near the centre of London, my head feels better and everything is sharply in contrast to the stormy night. The green of the trees is deep and varied. So, so green. It must rain a lot here, but it's not raining now. It's bright, hot and sunny. Eddie tells me that some days in August can be unbearable as far as heat goes. The Notting Hill Carnival usually falls on the hottest weekend of the summer, and that's today. I can already hear music in the distance. Eddie says it's important for me to stay awake until at least 9pm, even though I've missed a night's sleep, because that way I'll get over the jetlag quickly. He too wants me to have my head checked, but I hope he'll just forget about it. Right now, I'm so tired that I'm merely grateful to be on solid ground.

Beatrice meandered along Portobello Road with her cousin Edward Lock who, at the age of thirty-nine, was still a bachelor because, as he said, marriage is for a man and woman who want to raise a child, and then to start having fights with one another. "None of that for me," he said. "And besides, I like tall women and they don't like me."

Eddie was very short, barely five feet tall, Beatrice guessed, which was not much for a man. He was attractive, but compact and scrunched into very little body space. His face was kind, and Beatrice thought that many people might find him attractive, but he was so short that perhaps they didn't notice him. She loomed above him and felt slightly awkward as they strolled through Notting Hill, as Edward pointed out the sights of his neighbourhood.

"This part of West London was once full of people from the Caribbean," he said as he pointed to a tiny shop that sold fresh fruit juices. "But now," he waved his hand in the general direction of the boutiques, "it's frightfully trendy..."

Beatrice was enticed by the smells and sounds coming from the street. Eddie said that it was not always like this. At Carnival time the streets were full of vendors, performers, and more Caribbean people than usual. Beatrice couldn't believe she had not actually flown backwards and landed in the Caribbean again. Anything seemed possible after that flight. The street vendors were offering patties, curried goat and roti, soursop drinks and jerk chicken. And the music was loud, loud, as loud as in Trinidad on J'Ouvert morning or on Christmas morning in Georgetown, with the drums and Mother Sally doing her dance.

And there were crowds of people like those at home. African faces, Indian faces, mixed-up faces, all as though she'd never left. The only difference was that so many of these people had strong, proper English accents.

Eddie stopped in front of a store with vintage clothing and antiques. The clothes in the window were almost like costumes from another century. A bell above the door rang as he pushed it open and walked in, with Beatrice following him.

"Hey, love," Eddie said to another very short man who was ironing a long white dress on an ironing board at the rear of the store.

"Eddie ... you got her all right then? I thought you'd had enough of Carnival after last year... you said you were staying home!" came the response. Eddie approached his friend and, to

Beatrice's surprise, gave him a big hug and a kiss on the lips. She'd never seen two men kiss before.

"I can't really stay away, and this year I have an excuse," Eddie replied. "Richard, this is my second cousin from Guyana, Beatrice. Beatrice, Richard." Richard's head reached to just below Beatrice's shoulders.

"Pleasure to meet you, miss," Richard said gallantly, as he shook her hand. "You on holiday, are you?"

"Well, sort of a holiday, more like a journey," replied Beatrice.

"You've come at the best time, at least for these parts. Good weather, good fun. Welcome, welcome. Need any fancy dresses while you're here?" With a sweeping gesture of his hands he directed her eyes about the room to the beautiful ball gowns, jackets, furs and purses from a bygone era.

"I don't think so, I'm on a tight budget," she said politely while eyeing the clothing with desire. These were the clothes of movie stars, the costumes of great actresses from the golden age of movies. Her mind played a scene. She wore a long, flowing, chiffon dress that trailed behind her as she walked down a grand staircase and said to her awaiting butler, "I want to be alone!" She blinked the scene away and stared in awe at the dresses before her. A window display of bags and shoes drew her attention. Her eyes fixed on a pair of shining red patent leather shoes with a slight heel and sturdy soles.

"Found something you like?" asked Richard as he came up behind her with his quick, hoppy step.

"Wow, those are beautiful," she said, entranced.

"Try them on," he said, taking the red shoes from the window display.

"No, no, I couldn't," she began.

"Sure you can, Bea, why not?" said Eddie, also behind her.

Beatrice allowed Richard to slip the shoes onto her feet. Perfect fit. She loved them, and, though stylish, they were comfortable. They would glide her through streets in Europe, she thought. She felt like a movie star in them.

"That settles it," Eddie piped up as he took his wallet out of his back pocket.

"No, Eddie, you can't," Beatrice protested.

"Sure I can. I don't have any family of my own here, Bea, and you've just made my day by looking so great and so tall in those gorgeous shoes."

The two short men convened at the counter to settle payment for Eddie's gift. Beatrice stood looking at herself in the mirror. She twisted her legs this way and that to get a full view of the shoes. She would take them with her everywhere.

WWW.WORLDMAIL.COM

Felix

> I'm in London, writing you this from a shop on Oxford Street
> where rows and rows of computers are being used by what
> feels like hundreds of people. And there are more in the queue
> waiting for the next available terminal. London is crowded
> and a bit grimy, but full of fun.

> I was almost devoured by a human-sized lion during a
> carnival parade. No joke. Well, a bit of a joke. Standing beside
> the road watching a band on a parade float move by, I was
> frightened by an extremely loud blast near my ear. A roar
> from a wild beast louder than the pan music coming from the
> band. When I turned I saw a huge, fiercely-drawn lion face
> with a wild mane and bared teeth! To my relief the man-lion
> took off his costume head and smiled at me, then jumped off
> the float and began to talk to me. He's the first British person
> I've met other than Eddie and Richard, and even though at
> first he seemed very reserved, he has been very keen to talk
> to me. I think we'll become friends. Don't tell Mom and Dad,
> but he's been in prison before, in Ireland, but that was a long
> time ago and he was wrongly accused. He's shown me some
> of the more interesting and seedy sights of London, but has
> also filled in the gaps in my history education, all those times
> when I just wasn't listening at school. I never thought
> travelling would be such an education.

> In your last email you said you'd been to the interior with
> Dad. Lucky you. Did you take a riverboat? What snakes along
> the way? I thought you were supposed to be going to scout
> camp this year? Or are you sick and tired of that? Tell Mom I
> got her email and tell her not to fret about me so much! I'll
> write her again soon.

> Bea xxx

August 25

Dear Diary

After Sean took off his costume, I could see his kind face. My fear
disappeared. The band played on but Sean was off the float and
standing next to me, holding the life-like lion head mask under his
arm and looking at me with his piercing blue eyes.

"You're a one-off, you are..." he said, from behind me, in a lilt that
almost sang.

"Excuse me?" I asked. He was staring at me, and I was retreating,
shyly. I saw him glance down at my new red shoes, and I was
delighted that I'd let Eddie buy them for me.

"You're a one-off, unique, none other I've seen like you," he
explained as he looked up again. His voice was deep and calm.

I didn't respond, but I couldn't take my eyes off him, because he
was so good-looking. He had sandy blond hair and dazzling blue
eyes. His face was chiselled like the statue of someone famous.
But a scar that ran across his cheek like a railway track under his
left eye marred the perfection. With his penetrating gaze, there was
certainly something very interesting about him.

"You've not been here before, have you?" he said, and I realised
he was Irish.

"It's my first time," I said, wondering how he knew. Just then
another band was passing and the hollering and jumping-up around
the float made it impossible to continue our conversation. The
music was very loud, and people pushed through the crowd trying to
get a better look. I thought I was going to lose him in the swarm of
bodies, but then I felt a hand on my arm. He guided me out of the
crowd. I followed as he walked with his lion head still tucked under

his arms. We moved through the streets and ended up outside of the main carnival area.

"My name's Sean Walsh," he said as he looked around him, still trying to guide us to someplace more quiet.

"Beatrice Douglas," I said and heard my own accent.

"Where are you from?" he asked.

When I told him Guyana he smiled and grabbed my arm as we made our way through the press of bodies. I watched his shifting gaze through the crowd as we reached another corner. We entered a quiet café. What was I doing? How had I let him just take me over like that? Mom would have had conniptions if she'd seen me then, talking to a strange man. But there was something not so strange about him. He had a calm, familiar face, and such strength. Strength of character, that was probably what made me think of Mom in the first place. It's the same strength that I see in her when she's off doing her gardening or her work in the restaurant. Confidence that emanates from her body. In his body it made him walk proudly and forcefully through throngs of people.

In the café he said, "Look, I'll tell you right off, someone's out to get me, they always are, but don't worry, you'll be safe with me. No one's tried anything in years. You can trust me. And I know I can trust you. I'm never wrong about a face." He looked around again, afraid of being overheard.

"What are you talking about?" I asked, feeling suddenly as though I'd hooked up with a madman. And that's when he got into his whole story.

"Belfast," he said, again looking around. He ordered a coffee for himself, tea for me and we talked. Belfast was where all his troubles had begun. When he was a teenager he'd been involved with some militant friends who had talked to him about freedom and revolution and he became so convinced that he decided to write newspaper articles, letters and communiqués for the group. He made some deliveries and did some errands for them, but he didn't want to be involved in violence. Then one day soon after a very bad blast in the city, the English army came to his door and took him and his brother to jail. They weren't given a trial, weren't given any chance to defend themselves, just rounded up and locked up for a long, long time. The scar on his face he got in prison, but he didn't say how.

"I didn't set a bomb, and I didn't murder anyone," he said, with his eyes looking through me. I still couldn't figure out why he was telling me all this.

"Why are you telling me all of this?" I asked bluntly.

"Well..." he started, then hesitated. "I'm not entirely sure. I guess I just know faces when I see them. It's a talent I have. I know them and I know when to trust them. And your face just looks like that. Full of all sorts of stories, and all of them true."

I didn't know whether to be flattered or to be worried, but there was something about his face I trusted too.

"It must take courage to survive prison," I said.

"No, not at all. Freedom is what takes courage... and I'm not sure I have it any more," he said, shaking his head. He looked around again, nodding to a man in the café who met his eye.

He didn't say how long he'd been in prison, but I guess it was for a couple of years. He didn't go to school past the age of sixteen. His twentieth birthday is this month. "I was born in August, lion in the zodiac," he said and then held up the lion head that he'd placed on the table. He continued to remind me so much of Mom, who is also born this month, also a lion. His face is kind, like hers. But he has strong, masculine features.

"What are you doing here, Beatrice Douglas?" he asked finally.

I thought for a moment before answering. I felt like telling him about really wanting to be an actress in Hollywood, but it all sounded so foolish after his story, and I knew that something else was taking place on this trip, so all I said was "I'm not sure, really... just a journey..."

'You're in the right place. Lots of journeys have begun here. Even the one of your own family somewhere down the line. Big island, this, and all mixed up and confused about itself and where everyone belongs. Here there's just about everything you want, and old voices, old, old voices that come out of the stone. You been to Stonehenge?'

"No, not yet."

"Well, there and in other places, in Ireland, Scotland, and Wales, you can feel it. You hear an ancient whisper. The original people in Britain were worshippers of the sun, always searching. When they got here they thought they'd found the sun's end, and they prayed to the stone and they prayed to the dying light of December. They waited for something to tell them where go to next, but this is an island. They ended up building stones and altars to the sun that never came. Brave, they were. Brave and waiting. Maybe that's why people later went to your part of the world. Couldn't wait for the sun any longer."

I pictured Druids dancing around fire and making sacrifices to stone gods. I looked up at Sean and he was grinning, as though he could read my mind.

"I can read faces," he said, and then I was sure he'd read my mind. "You should see the rest of Britain. It's a mystery and masterpiece both in one. I could show you," he added, and I was hooked. What was I doing? Was this dangerous? Even if it was, there was something that told me I had to do it, had to see him again to be shown things that I could never have imagined. Sean was full of secrets, that was for sure, and the way he talked about ancient things made me feel he knew about the older, darker side of life. Maybe that is what I am here for.

I had been planning to stay in London and to see some plays and to spend long afternoons in the cinemas watching movies, but when Sean said, "I'm going to the Scottish Highlands in a couple of days," I knew that I would join him.

Oh diary, things are so interesting...

A few days later Beatrice was on an overnight train to Inverness, trying to sleep in her seat. She had kicked off her red shoes, and her head was resting on her backpack. She'd been obliged to explain her change of plans to Eddie and to ask him to cover for her.

"What do you want me to tell your Mom when she calls on Sunday?" Eddie had asked her.

"Tell her I'm fine and that I've got an opportunity to see Scotland. I'll call her myself when I get there." Eddie gave her a disbelieving look. "I promise, Eddie, I will. Please help me on this one," she pleaded. Richard was sitting at the kitchen table and the two short men looked at each other anxiously, feeling protective of Beatrice. Then Richard nodded as if to say he thought it would be all right.

"Thanks Richard," Beatrice said happily and hurried over to kiss him on both cheeks. She did the same to Eddie.

"You be careful, Bea... you're not going to do anything foolish, are you?"

"Of course not, Eddie," she assured him. But of course she had left out a few details about her trip, that she was going with Sean, and they were going to visit friends of his she had no idea about. And she said nothing about Sean's background. She didn't want to worry them unnecessarily.

Richard and Eddie had cooked Beatrice a beautiful going-away meal of Dover sole and roast vegetables, with delicious English trifle for dessert.

"You have to go to Africa on your trip, Bea," Eddie said as they were washing up.

"Oh yes?" She was puzzled to hear the same suggestion that Linda had made at the airport. "Why?"

"Because Africa is where it all began, isn't it? The first humans can be traced back to one woman, Lucy, the first Homo sapiens. Her bones were found in Africa."

Beatrice thought about this fact as she put the plates in the cupboard. She wondered if she should ask the two men what they knew about ancient voices in stone that Sean had mentioned. But she decided against it.

Now she was on a train, watching Sean sleep curled up in his seat with his arms wrapped around himself to keep warm. Beatrice pictured him on a cold prison floor, the guard coming to kick him... she shivered at the thought of that movie and stopped it there.

When they arrived in Inverness, they took a coach to the Glen Affric Lodge. The sight of Loch Affric was exhilarating, with a breeze rippling its surface, the boulders at its shore and a marshy inlet in which stood a majestic heron. Evergreens and oaks rose up around the land as it peaked into a ridge. Behind the ridge the hills were higher still, and beyond them, mountains. Sean told her that if they climbed to the top of the second ridge they could see the highest mountain in Scotland, Ben Nevis, and its range of jagged peaks.

Inside the stately lodge, piano music played softly in one of the upper rooms, but the rest of the house was still and quiet. Beatrice explored the ground floor, impressed by its splendour.

Whoever had lived here, or whoever could afford to hire this lodge, certainly had privilege.

"Anybody here?" Sean called out. Someone came running down the stairs: a tall woman with strawberry blonde hair and freckles, older than Beatrice and dressed in hip, wide trousers and a midriff tee-shirt.

"Sean, you made it, what a blessing!" she said as she hugged him and they kissed each other.

"Rachel, this is Beatrice. She's from Guyana, and when we met in London I knew she had to come up here," he said, standing aside to let Rachel shake Beatrice's hand.

"Did he tell you he could read it in your face? That's his trick; he tells everyone that, that's how he snagged me!" she said and gave Sean a loving pinch on the side.

"Don't listen to her, she's jealous of my gift..."

"Great to have you here, Beatrice, come in," Rachel added.

"Thank you," Beatrice said shyly.

Rachel showed her upstairs to a bedroom that would be hers for the next few nights. Beatrice unpacked, taking out her trainers and putting them on, leaving her red shoes at the foot of the bed.

Downstairs, she walked out of the door and caught a glimpse of the view from the south side of the house. Breathtaking, glistening water and green hills, bordered by a tree-lined ridge. Several people were gathered down at the dock. At the sight of them Beatrice became nervous, worried she wouldn't know what to say to them, but she took a deep breath and walked towards the loch.

"Beatrice, come and meet everyone," said Sean warmly.

She was introduced to ten new people, all of whom were in their twenties, unique-looking, well-educated and cultured. Beatrice felt intimidated.

But they were talking about movies.

Her ears tuned in. Excitement rushed through her. She sat down on the dock with them as they sipped tea and chatted. She discovered they were a production team of filmmakers, taking a break after shooting their first film. Film students at Bristol University, they had decided to get together to produce a script written by Rachel and Sean. Everyone had had a role in the filming, and now they were discussing the next steps.

Beatrice was awestruck. Here were people actually making movies, not just watching them and dreaming of being in one some day. She didn't know what to say when they asked her what she did, except that she was taking some time off before deciding. She felt foolish for her childish ideas. Ever since that ghastly plane ride, everything seemed different.

"We're going on a long walk up the ridge tomorrow. Are you up for it?" Sean asked her as the group broke up to go their individual ways, some opting for a boat ride to the beach at the other end of the loch, others opting for naps.

"Sure, of course," Beatrice said. The way Sean looked at her made her nervous, but she knew it wasn't a lusty look. It was a look that said, "you're interesting and I want to know more about you." It was the examining look he gave to all new faces.

"Great, we'll leave early in the morning, but tonight there's dinner, and lots of fun, I hope. You relax and do whatever you like, take a walk around. There's a trail behind the house. You can walk without too much climbing, and it goes on for miles," he told her.

Beatrice decided she would hang about on the lawn and catch up on her letters home. She felt more content than she had been in a long, long time.

```
Dear Stephanie,
Will wonders never cease? I'm in Scotland. The
Highlands, to be exact, and it's crisp and
green, treed and full of music. I hadn't really
planned on coming here, but I'm so glad I did.
Being here has reminded me of my own Scottish
heritage, my surname, and the more invisible
parts of me. Our family pays little attention
to our Scottish ancestry, not knowing exactly
the lineage to follow. We tend to be singled
out for the Amerindian, Chinese, and African.
It's interesting to feel that this is part of
me too.
    The best thing is that I've met fascinating
people, all from different places in Britain.
And, Steph, they make movies! They're not
```

Hollywood people; they're serious and arty. I don't know what their movie is about, but they talk about politics and culture, and they analyse films and know the history of film, especially foreign-language films. They refer to movies by their directors, and I feel like a country booboo in their company. There's so much I don't know about acting or movies, and yet that's the only thing I want to be involved in. Everyone I've met has been kind, and they ask me about home, my family, and seem especially interested in the politics in Guyana. Unfortunately I'm even too ignorant about that to contribute to the conversation. Daddy was right; I should have studied harder.

The most intriguing person I've met so far is Sean. Girl, you would die to see him. Gorgeous, and not stupidy like the boys at home (even Raj - sorry, but it's true. Raj plays the fool too much!). Sean is not an egomaniac like Dante in Miami. He's kind and gentle, and he looks at me like I'm the best thing he's ever seen in his life.

He has strange outbursts, though - feelings and ideas and things that just spill out of his mouth unexpectedly. His smile reminds me of my Mom's, all creased and crooked. He's a writer. He wrote the script that the others filmed. His girlfriend is as nice as he is, and they talk on late into the night sitting on the dock. In one of Sean's strange bursts he said, "OK, so I'm afraid of dying, what wrong with that?" I didn't know how to answer him. He thinks his life will be short, but I think he may be paranoid. I'll tell you the details another time.

Last night we had a small fete. Delicious food cooked by Rachel, Sean's girlfriend. We ate out under the stars, and after dinner one of the boys (whose family is from Bangladesh, but he sounds to me more English than the English), started to play the guitar. The others joined in, singing all kinds of songs and then someone took up a fiddle and someone else a flute! Rachel started to dance and was so happy she fell down the hill towards the dock. We all laughed when we knew she hadn't been hurt. I saw Sean and Rachel snuggled together at the end of the table, and I couldn't help but be just a bit envious.

Anyway, girl, it has been an eye-opening adventure up here in the highlands where my great, great, great grandfather might have come from. Where else would I have gotten the Douglas name? Tomorrow we're going climbing up the ridge to the top. I hope my legs hold out! Will write again soon.

Lots of love,
Bea xx

Beatrice gripped the edge of the mossy rock in front of her and inched further, crawling almost vertically up the side of the ridge. Afraid to look down, she shot her gaze towards Sean and Rachel, who were up ahead of her. The other climbers had turned back when the climb became steep, the grassy knolls replaced by rock and dirt paths and then finally a sheer rock underfooting. They didn't want to risk slipping down the rock, but these brave three had decided to push on to the top, if only just to catch sight of Ben Nevis. What have I got myself into? Beatrice wondered. She was hoping someone might yell out "CUT!" and she'd be magically transported out of the scene and into a hot bath. But this was real. She was not in her movie imagination. She had come this far because Sean's bravado the night before had inspired her. "Makes you feel freer than a bird to be up there," he had said. There was something about him that challenged her to seek out things she'd never done before.

"And you can hear the stone whisper," he added.

But now on the slope even he seemed terrified. His face was ashen with fright. Beatrice knew that Sean had a kind of inner knot he wanted to untie, and that he thought he was a coward. It had something to do with his time in prison, but she couldn't imagine what it might be.

Rachel made it to the top of the ridge before Beatrice or Sean, and she began to wave. The others who had stayed at the bottom waved back at her. Then she waved more urgently, jumping up and down and shouting something at Beatrice and Sean. They couldn't make out what she was saying. Beatrice assumed she was revelling in her triumph at reaching the summit of the ridge.

Sean was climbing ahead of Beatrice, when suddenly, in a false step, his foot slipped from the rock. His other foot reached forward in an attempt to balance his body, but it too slipped on the edge. His hands couldn't hold the ledge in front of him, and he began to slide down the rock on his chest. As he slid, he grasped frantically for something to hold on to, but each grasp was lost to the weight and speed of his falling body. He plunged down the ridge. His body hit a small mound, which slowed him down and flipped him over, but he continued to tumble down, picking up speed, bumping into rocks and mounds in his path. Beatrice screamed. She could hear only her own scream, but could see the open mouths of the others at the bottom, watching in horror as Sean's body tumbled towards them.

Beatrice couldn't move. Sean finally reached a flat part of the ridge and his body rolled to a stop. The others rushed towards him. When Beatrice looked up she saw Rachel coming down the ridge towards her. Beatrice was numb with shock and unable to head up or down, barely able to breathe. She stared at the rock and grass in front of her. Time passed as she concentrated on breathing. Suddenly she felt a hand on her shoulder.

Rachel was beside her. She held Beatrice's shoulders and helped her ease back down the slope by forcing her to squat and slide gently on her feet. Every few feet Rachel turned to touch Beatrice's shoulder as they descended. They finally made their way to the group and to Sean who was sitting on the grass catching his breath, holding his side.

"I can't believe it, I can't believe it," he kept repeating, shaking his head.

"What's amazing is that you aren't dead," said the guitar player.

"I can't believe it, I can't believe it," Sean continued. Beatrice saw terror in his eyes and noticed that his scar was more prominent than ever, almost throbbing. She knew there was more than just the fall in Sean's fear.

Back at the lodge he was quiet, looking out to the ridge from the dock while he nursed his cuts and bruises. Miraculously, he was not seriously injured. Apparently, as they both found out too late, Rachel had been shouting at them to abandon the ascent. She could see from where she stood that there was loose rock. She had been waving them off, not on. Beatrice was dismayed at how they could have mistaken Rachel's signals. Sean was clearly in shock. Rachel was looking after him and trying to remain calm, but at one point in the evening tears streamed down her face.

That evening, the group was unusually quiet. Most of them turned in just after supper, all a little shaken by the risks they had taken and by the power of the mountains. Beatrice went down to meet Sean on the dock as the sun was setting and the sky appeared to have been wrapped in orange gauze.

"I'm thinking of moving on," she said to him as she sat down. The words made her sad, mostly because of the thought that she would leave her new friend. But it was their meeting that had spurred her to greater challenges. She wanted more. She wanted a place so different from Guyana she would have no choice but to experience something fantastic.

Sean didn't look up. He stared out at the loch and sky. "Magic hour, they call this in the film business..." he said finally. He turned and gazed at her. "Where will you go?"

"France, first, then who knows, but I have to use my time to see as much as possible."

"Do you speak French?" he asked, simply, not surprised by her decision.

"Only what I learned in school," she confessed. He was deep in thought for a few seconds and then gave that knowing look again.

"Need a guide?" he asked with a smile.

"What do you mean?" she returned, feeling a rush of hope.

"Well, it's a good opportunity for me. I want to get away, to write something new. I think I have a story. About death. And I speak French," he said, looking at her with a gentle question in his eyes.

Beatrice was frightened at the mention of death. Sean certainly had a way of getting to the point. "You're not going die on me in France are you?" she teased. He looked uncomfortable, and she wondered if she'd made a bad joke. "It might be expensive in France," she threw in with a smile. "I'm meant to look up a friend of my Mom's in Paris. But..."

"If you don't want me to come, I won't, but..."

"Oh, no, of course I do. But ... won't you miss Rachel?"

"Rachel and I have an understanding. We let each other go when we need to. We always come back to each other."

Beatrice hesitated. She knew Sean's company meant excitement, but she wondered if she shouldn't try to travel alone. As the moon rose and glistened on the loch, she could feel adventure beckoning her.

"Well, I don't know if I'm any good at world travel, especially in a foreign language, and I do manage to run over nasty women's feet with my luggage cart. There's one already vex with me..."

She was stalling, but she knew deep down what her answer would be, and so did he, because a smile grew on his face. "Let's leave tomorrow!" she said and put her hand out to shake his. He took her hand gently and shook it. His scar seemed to glow in the faint dusk light.

Paris, France

WWW.WORLDMAIL.COM

Mom, Dad and Felix

> Bonjour! I'm in Paris, the city of lights.

> I didn't know a big city could be so beautiful. I've walked
> down the Champs Élysées, seen Montmartre, and tonight I'm
> even going to go to the opera. Will wonders never cease! Any
> morsels of French I learned in school are of little use to me
> here, where people look at me strangely when I open my
> mouth and out comes some patois or confused Franglais. The
> Parisians are, I have to say, a bit "proper," but I've also met
> some really helpful people. They seem very proud of their
> city, and maybe that's why they've got the reputation for
> being snobbish. But then again, to me, any place where you
> can go sliding into droppings of dog dung on the pavement
> doesn't seem overly precious! I've had my share of mushy
> mis-steps. Yesterday I had to wash my shoes off in a
> fountain. It must be why there's so much perfume here!

> How are things there? What is the latest gossip at the
> restaurant? How is everyone I know?

> I'll write again from the next available Internet café.

> Lots of Love, Bea xx

September 10

Dear Diary

I've neglected you, forgive me. It's just that now I have someone to talk to and share my experiences with. Actually, I now have two people, but let me get to that in good time.

Sean said goodbye to Rachel, and he and I left Scotland and returned to London for a few days, where we booked tickets and bought a French dictionary and a guidebook. I stayed with Eddie. Really enjoyed my time there. He and Richard are, well, sort of married - not legally, but they are life partners to each other. I was surprised at first. I don't think Mommy or any of her family knows about their partnership, but it made perfect sense given how well matched they are. It was wonderful to see them so happy together. The two of them really make me laugh. They like to "take the piss," as they say in England. They're both very short, and both have big, hearty laughs that resound through the room. Sometimes Eddie is brought to tears by laughing so hard at Richard's ridiculous puns. They sing a lot together too - show tunes from the London theatre and pop songs.... *Mama Mia...* with the accompanying dance moves. I was sorry I had to leave them and their hilarity. But after Scotland, meeting Sean's filmmaker friends, and after Sean's fall, I knew I had to keep moving.

Sean is a risk-taker, a daredevil. He talks to strange people and dares me to take chances too. Before we left London, he took me to the Westminster Bridge, where he climbed onto the railing and did a dancing and singing act that frightened the life out of me. Then he held his nose as if he were about to plunge into the Thames. I screamed, and he pulled back. I know he was only arsing around, but it gave me such a fright I started to be worried about travelling with him. But I threw my caution over that bridge instead, and off we went.

We decided not to go on the Eurostar through the channel tunnel, because we wanted to experience the white cliffs of Dover, the sea, and Normandy the way folks did before the speed of the trains. We took a train to Portsmouth and the overnight ferry to Le Havre. The ferry ride was a rolly trip, since the weather had been bad at sea for a few days. We didn't stay out on the deck. We sat inside, trying to stay amused and comfortable. Sean kept notes on the new script he's writing about courage and death. He did push-ups right there in the open space of the passenger deck, not caring if anyone thought it was strange. I watched him with envy, all that confidence, and the lack of the self-consciousness that plagues me.

I was tired and wanted to sleep. I squirmed in my seat, fearing a night like the one I'd had on the plane to London. When sleep didn't come, I decided to explore the ship. It was just before dawn, and without bothering with my shoes, I walked to the elevator. When the door opened, I stepped inside and read the panel of floor buttons. A small sign on the panel said: "No unaccompanied teenagers allowed in the elevator." I held the door from closing and quickly jumped out of the lift, afraid I might get caught and perhaps reprimanded. I couldn't understand why I wasn't allowed in the elevator. I am a teenager, technically, still in my teens, but here I am travelling on my own around the world! It didn't make sense to me that I wasn't allowed in an elevator, so I went into the washroom, put on make-up, took my red shoes out of my knapsack, and slipped them on. I looked more mature, and up in the lift I went!

Out on the deck, as the sun was beginning to glow just below the horizon, I saw a young man in the oddest clothes, juggling three batons like skinny bowling pins. He was very good, and the batons flew faster and faster with each toss. Dressed in yellow tights, a striped shirt, with two cameras hanging from his neck, he looked like he belonged in a circus. His gold suede shoes had pointy toes, and he wore a floppy striped hat. The thought of a circus made my mind race. I stood watching him and imagined my own act. I'd be the woman who gets sawed in half by her partner. I saw myself there under the big top. The lights are low, the audience hushed as my sawing partner begins. It's not an ordinary saw. He lifts it from the floor and pulls a cord. The buzz reverberates through the circus tent. It's a buzz saw of startling proportions. The audience lets out a gasp. My partner moves in closer to me, confined in my box with my toes wiggling wildly at the end of it. He brings the blade down to the box. Closer and closer. The sound is getting louder. I am searching with my hand for the latch that will lower me away from the blade's path. I struggle. I begin to panic. I can't find the latch! The saw is penetrating the wood. My hands do a desperate search and clutching. Still nothing!

The blade is approaching my tummy! I scream but he doesn't hear me. I scream and scream and scream!

"What's the matter?" said a panicked voice, suddenly beside me.

I came back to reality and realised that I had screamed right there on the deck of the ship as the sun was beginning to peek up over the horizon.

"Oh, nothing, nothing, excuse me, I was just thinking..." I said to the juggler.

"Well whatever it was, don't think it again. Obviously not good for you," and then he held up his small camera and was about to click a photograph of me.

"Wait a minute!" I yelled, and held my hand up in front of his camera to block the shot. What was going on? Who was this fellow?

"Sorry, bad habit. I forget that people don't like that. Will you still talk to me?" he asked, looking contrite and almost on the verge of tears. At this point I really thought he was an odd one.

"My name is Christopher, my real name, that is. But in the circus they used to call me Du Larme – it's French for tear. I had a bit of a reputation." He tipped his striped hat and held out his hand.

"Beatrice," I said, shaking his hand, feeling drawn to his oddness.

He was a young man of about my age, I guessed. Asian, very tall and very thin. We sat on the deck and chatted until the sun came up. He told me that his ancestors were from China but he had been born in London. When he finished school his father wanted him to work in his business, a restaurant supply store, but he wanted to be in the circus or to go to art school to become a photographer. His father would allow neither, so he worked in the business for a few months and then escaped. He literally ran away from everyone he'd ever known, and he joined a circus. He learned to juggle and to swallow fire and swords. After a few months he fell in love with the flying trapeze artist. They had their first kiss, their first long night together talking until dawn, and she promised to see him again. They spent a few intensely romantic months together, until one day his father found him and begged him to return home to London, claiming that he couldn't run the business without him. Christopher was racked with family guilt, and he returned for his father's sake. But he was so unhappy there that after one year he left again. He found out that the circus was in Belgium, and with a full and happy heart he had decided he would ask the trapeze flyer to marry him. However, when he got to Belgium he found out that she'd left the circus to marry a businessman she had met in the audience in Berlin. They were now expecting their first child. Christopher's heart was shattered. He couldn't remain in the circus, tortured by her memory. He started to roam. Now he was travelling to France to look for romance, to find his heart's true love in the woman of his dreams, and to try to forget the trapeze artist.

"There's only one true way to happiness, and that's through love," he said, gazing out to the land we could see in the distance. Tears began to stream down his face, and I understood then why the circus people had nicknamed him. He turned back to me and wiped his face with the sleeve of his shirt. He looked intensely at me, from head to foot.

"Nice shoes, Beatrice. Staying in France long?" he asked, as though shaken quickly out of his sadness by the sight of my shoes.

"I don't really know yet," I said, then looked down at my feet. When I looked up he had put his hand to my ear and, suddenly, in his fingers appeared a flower. He offered it to me like a gesture of love. I was stunned and could say nothing, could only take the flower and thank him, wondering how he did it and thinking again how odd he was.

He came down in the elevator with me to meet Sean, who stared at him. Sean examined Christopher's face, looking for its individual secret. Then he said, "Ah, broken heart," and Christopher began to cry again. Sean put his arm around him and invited him to sit down. The two of them seemed to hit it off instantly. Christopher showed Sean his juggling and magic, and Sean showed Christopher how to make knots with the rope from one of the life preservers. Christopher exclaimed at the successful tying of each knot, as though it was the best magic he'd ever seen. Christopher reminds me a lot of my brother Felix, the same wide, open and loving face, and after a few hours speaking with him I had a twinge of missing my little bratty brother. Christopher is a bit hotheaded like Felix, not at all reserved like the British. He said he thought he'd be more at home in France. I admire his flamboyance – highlighted by his passion and his wild and colourful clothes.

The three of us left the ferry and took a coach into Le Havre, an ugly city, if the truth were told. The old buildings were bombed in the war and the new ones are rather ... well, ugly, and so we took the train out of Le Havre in a hurry and ended up in Paris late in the afternoon, checking into a youth hostel on Boulevard de Strasbourg.

Paris. Every cliché about it is true. And for that it's magic. We walked a lot, and it was very hot, but also very beautiful. Christopher wore a long skirt instead of trousers, and Sean teased him endlessly about it, but Christopher said it was the one piece of clothing he felt most comfortable in. We sat by fountains and visited the Louvre, but it was too crowded for me, so I left quickly and waited on the steps for the other two. We made our way through the city, gazing at its elegance.

In front of the Centre Pompidou we watched street performers – some of them I couldn't understand because they spoke very fast French. Suddenly there was another crowd gathering around us, and I realised that Christopher had pulled out his batons and fire sticks and was doing his act for the crowd. He was wonderful. He would perform a trick or a stunt and take a photograph of the crowd's reactions. They laughed and clapped, and I found myself on the verge of tears. I think it was then that I started to miss everyone from home even more.

I wasn't the only one who cried that day. In the evening, Mommy's friend who works for the High Commission gave me, Sean, and Christopher tickets to the Opera at Bastille, where we saw "La Traviata." After the performance, Christopher wept and wept and kept repeating, "Oh, so tragic, so beautiful..." His eyes disappeared under their puffy lids. Sean made fun of him, telling him not to be so sentimental and to buck up, but I just held his hand as the lights came up in the opera house. He really is sentimental, like Felix.

When I first left Georgetown, all I wanted to do was go straight to Hollywood and take my plunge into stardom. But now, these sights and sounds have dazzled me in a way I don't quite know how to understand. I find myself thinking about things I thought I was finished with when I left school. My chest feels open and vulnerable to the pulses of the world. Nothing is as I had expected it, but it's much better. Europe isn't shiny and clean like a postcard. It's gritty and dowdier than on television. And I never expected to meet so many people. What would Stephanie say if she could see me travelling with these two men? "You courtin' danger like a fool!"

probably. None of this feels dangerous. I feel like I've known the two of them my whole life.

Tomorrow we're going to do something different, off the beaten track of the tourist parade. We're going to a market in Belleville, the Arab quarter of the city that Sean has heard about.

Outside the youth hostel, Christopher held up one of his two cameras, this one a Polaroid that would give him an instant image. He snapped a photograph of a beautiful woman in the street. Her yellow dress clung to her curves, and her high-heeled shoes made her tall and model-like, willowy and entrancing. Her long, flowing brown hair shone in the sunlight, and even Beatrice felt the pull of her beauty.

The photograph shot out of the camera and took its time developing, with Christopher staring at it as the image materialised. He stood with it in his hands, his back up against the wall of a building, looking very sad.

"What's the matter, lad?" Sean asked him. "You look terrified."

"No, not terrified," said Christopher choking back a tear. "I'm just sure I'll never find her, that's all."

"Find who?" Beatrice asked.

"*Her!*" he answered emphatically, raising his arm and pointing nowhere in particular, making the tassels on his cowboy shirt shake back and forth. "You know, *her*, the woman of my dreams. Here I am in Paris, the most romantic city in the world, and I still haven't found her."

"But we've been here just two days, Christopher," Beatrice said, trying to make light of it.

"It's not the amount of time, it's just that I don't think she's here, or anywhere. My parents always said I should marry a Chinese girl. They even wanted to choose one for me. That's another reason I ran away. But now I don't know, maybe they're right. Maybe I should do what they want..." he said sadly.

Beatrice was surprised to hear such resignation from someone as dynamic as Christopher. She shivered at the thought of what it would mean if her parents thought they should dictate whom she might one day marry. She put her hand on Christopher's shoulder but couldn't think of anything to say.

The three friends went down the stairs into the Metro station. The air was heavy with the smell of urine and the warm mustiness of the people who slept there at night. Being underground sent the three friends into the private retreat of their thoughts. Beatrice marvelled at how alike they were. Their varying backgrounds made little difference, except superficially. When they surfaced in Belleville, the market was in full swing with bright colours and buzzing sounds, and the three of them smiled as one. They strolled along the lanes, examining stalls of vegetables and fruit.

Christopher wore the headphones of his portable CD player over his striped hat. Music from *La Traviata* leaked out as he photographed a row of vegetables in a small, well-kept stall. He carefully set up the shot of aubergines laid out beside perfectly placed onions. What was he seeing, Beatrice asked herself? He was a curiosity to her.

"*Et vous, mademoiselle, quelque chose pour vous?*" came a voice from behind the counter. The woman looked at her with a kind, gap-toothed smile that seemed so familiar that Beatrice could have sworn she was someone from Guyana. But this woman was a stranger who wanted her to buy something. Beatrice picked up a row of dates and asked in her best French how much they were.

"*Trois Euros,*" said the gap-toothed woman.

Beatrice paid for them. While handing Beatrice her change the woman said:

"You have the same as my daughter," in broken English.

"The same?" Beatrice questioned.

"Yes, you have the same as my daughter," and the woman gestured with her hand running up and down in front of her body, meaning that Beatrice resembled her daughter.

"Oh, I see," Beatrice said and smiled broadly, taking her change.

"*Merci Madame.*"

"*Merci ma fille,*" said the woman as she turned to another customer. Beatrice was touched to have been called daughter by a perfect stranger.

It was an odd feeling to be recognised by someone from an entirely different culture. In Mexico it had felt similar, and also slightly confusing. What did it mean to look like you were something you weren't? Is that what being an actress would be like? Did blood have any real significance at all?

Loud yelling, in English, shook Beatrice out of her thoughts.

"He took my wallet – I know he did!" came a woman's loud American accent. Beatrice turned around and saw a short woman with wild red hair running after a young boy through the market. The woman circled and came back to the stall where Beatrice and her friends stood watching.

"Can't anybody here speak English?" the woman said in a booming voice.

The three friends looked at each other. Christopher was about to speak up when Beatrice shushed him. She recognised the curly red hair of the woman from the airport in London. It was the woman whose feet she had run into with her cart.

"Don't say anything, Chris, she's a nasty one... I've already had one run-in with her," she whispered to Christopher. He looked confused. The three friends stayed silent while the American woman walked through the market complaining that the boy had stolen her wallet.

"Look, what kind of place is this? Ripping off a well-paying customer. Who's responsible here? I want to talk to the person in charge!" she hollered to one man, but the man obviously understood nothing she was saying, or he pretended not to. The woman became more frustrated and angrier by the second.

Suddenly a scuffle at the far end of the market was followed by gunshots. Then a small explosion. Beatrice felt a hand on her arm pulling her away. She turned to see Sean also grab Christopher, dragging them both towards the other side of the street.

"I know a bomb when I hear it," he said, sounding more Irish than ever. The three of them started to run. Crouched in an alley a few streets away, Sean told them about the recent clashes between local community gangs and the police. The cultural tension in the quarter had increased random violence, just as in Ireland. Each incident escalated the possibility of another.

"It gets to the point where every murmur feels attached to a short fuse, ready to explode," he said.

When things seemed calm again, they walked back towards the Metro. The American woman, who had caught the young Arab boy, was at the corner. She was trying to drag the boy towards the police station, but he squirmed in her grasp and kicked her shin. The woman didn't let go, but started crying, mumbling to herself, 'This just isn't fair, this just isn't fair...' The boy pleaded with her in Arabic. Finally an older man arrived and grabbed the boy. The man pushed the American woman to the side, forcing her back to slam against the wall of a building. The violence made Beatrice queasy. The woman started hollering.

"How dare you! I'll have you both arrested and imprisoned immediately!"

She ran towards the boy and grabbed him again, this time by his ear, but he squirmed out of her grasp and ran away. The woman was left flabbergasted, stamping her foot on the pavement. Beatrice felt confused and wondered who, between the two, had been the worse treated.

In the Metro, Beatrice felt restless again. Perhaps she needed to avoid homesickness by moving on to her next destination. She wanted to get out of big cities for a while and to go somewhere near the sea. She decided to test out her idea on Christopher and Sean.

"I don't know if you still want to come with me, but I was thinking of staying in France for a little while longer – so you might meet the woman of your dreams yet, Chris, if you decide to come – but I thought I might go to the south. To Cannes. I want to see what it's like, since it's where the biggest film festival in the world is held every year."

"But it's over, Beatrice. It takes place in May," said Sean.

"I know, I know, but since I'm already here in France I'd like to say I've been."

"Cool. The Riviera – very romantic," said Christopher.

Sean looked into his hands on his lap for a moment and the other two watched him as he weighed his choices. He looked up and stared them both in the eyes, intensely as he had the first time they met. Beatrice felt uncomfortable and saw trouble lurking in his stare, but then he smiled.

"OK, I'm in," he said matter-of-factly.

Cannes, France

Dear Stephanie, Bonjour from the Riviera!
No movie stars here at the moment, at
least none that we can find. Lots of people with a lot of money. Last
night we went out for dinner and I was dressed up, in my fanciest
dress, the beautiful locket you gave me at the airport, and the red
shoes I got in London. I tried to look chic but failed miserably. It's
much too expensive for us here. (When I say "us" I mean me and
the two new friends I've made.) My friend Christopher thinks we
should go to China. I wasn't planning to go there, but it might be a
good idea, and Christopher has family we can stay with in Hong
Kong. Imagine me, like Suzie Wong in the old movie!
Girl, the boys in France look sweet, sweet. You'd be in your
element. Will write again soon,

Bea xx

September 15

Oh, Diary, where to go from here? Cannes is beautiful, but I haven't
been able to understand what it has to do with movies. Sean says
that it's very different when the film festival is on. Last night I
imagined my life as a star, in my red shoes, as I clicked down the
croissette and listened to the sounds and chatter from the chic
people in the cafés. Do I want to be walking up a velvet carpet one
day with all eyes on me? Everything I believed is shifting. I thought I
was one thing, but now I don't know any more. I thought that being
an actress in Hollywood interpreting other people's stories was the
only thing there was to be, but now I think that I have my own stories
to tell. I am homesick and want the familiar faces of Felix, Mom, and

Dad, but I also want something new. Part of me wants to sit on the sea wall and talk endlessly with Stephanie and for us to imagine our futures with cars and money and handsome men. Another part wants something much more challenging than that. My mind has been working overtime.

Christopher is convinced he should go to China, to see if his heart's desire is possibly there. He has persuaded me to go with him, and even Sean has now decided to join us. Christopher has reminded me that I have Chinese blood and that I should get a look at where some of my ancestors are from. But Diary, who am I?

Beijing, China

"Tinkle, tinkle, tinkle, rattle, rattle, tinkle…" the growing noises spread through the morning as Beatrice slowly climbed out of sleep. Dawn. The small hotel room overlooked a busy street, and the sounds heralded the start of a new working day.

This early, thought Beatrice? She was jetlagged, having left Paris in the afternoon and after a long flight arrived in Beijing the next day. She, Sean and Christopher had walked around in a daze, marvelling at the distinct difference of China. It was like nowhere else they had been or could have imagined.

Beatrice jumped out of bed and looked out of the window. The wide avenues near Tiananmen Square were swarming with people and activity. The rising "tinkle, tinkle, rattle, rattle…" was the sound of wave after wave of jingling bicycles. Bicycles like an army of ants. Men and women dressed in plain, simple city clothes were riding to work, some towing children on their handlebars. Men in a tiny park across from the hotel were performing the slow-motion dance of Tai Chi. Beatrice had seen Chinese people in London performing the same floating movements in Hyde Park one early morning. But now, she was in China! The thought thrilled her. In her film mind she was Susie Wong walking quickly down the street in a tight dress, the men whistling at her while she paid them no mind. Susie would dance tonight. Dance until she could no longer stand up. CUT: Take Two. What was it about the part of Susie Wong that was right for her? How would this leg of her journey help her account for the thing inside her that kept asking who am I? Beatrice's great-great-great grandfather had been Chinese, recruited to Guyana as a labourer to work in rice paddies in Berbice. How was she herself connected to this country?

Soon after she was dressed and feeling safe in her red shoes, there was a knock at her door. Beatrice opened it to see the smiling faces of Sean and Christopher.

"Well, here we are, do you believe it?" Christopher said, excited and more at ease than the whole time they had been in France.

"We have lots to do. I want to see the Forbidden City," said Sean. He paused, looked at Christopher and roared at the top of his lungs, frightening his friend and backing him up against the wall of the corridor. Beatrice wondered what on earth had got into him, but she was happy that he was his lively self.

"Okay, well, let's go to see what there is to see..." Beatrice said, joining in their enthusiasm.

They made their way in the wave of people headed along the cobbled roadway from Tiananmen to the main gate of the magnificent Forbidden City. The Wu Men gate had been built as far back as the fifteenth century, and Sean touched one of its railings as though it were an apparition. At the next gate, a pair of oversized bronze lions stood guard. Sean crawled up beside one of the lions and asked Christopher to take his picture as he let out another monstrous lion's roar into the hazy morning.

They toured the gated city, its wooden dwellings with clay roofs upswept in elaborate decoration. Carved dragons adorned the roof corners. Painted mosaics lined the eaves. They wandered through the Hall of Complete Harmony to a long stairway upon which there was a railing packed with sculpted dragons, carved from a single slab of marble, weighing more than two hundred tons.

"Will you look at what labourers had to pull on their backs to please the Emperor," Sean said, pointing at the massive slab.

"But then the artists got to sculpt it, Sean... look at this..." said Christopher as he ran his hands over the smooth wings of one of the dragons. Suddenly he jumped back with a scream!

"Oh my god!" he cried.

"What is it?" asked Beatrice, approaching the dragon he had touched.

"Did you see that?" he asked both of them.

"See what?" Sean returned.

"It opened its eyes and winked at me!"

Sean and Beatrice looked at each other and broke into a grin.

"Ya, well, at least something is winking at you, but I did hold out hope it would be a girl!" Sean teased.

"I'm not kidding, really. I saw it. It opened its eyes, which were fiery orange, and then one eyelid closed in a quick wink. I really didn't imagine it, I'm telling you. You have to believe me," Christopher defended. He took off his striped hat and looked into it, searching for something there, perhaps magic that he'd not been aware of.

Sean looked at Beatrice again, and he was about to tease Christopher some more, but she gestured a "pay-no-attention" to him with her hands.

"Let's keep moving. There's still a lot to see today," Beatrice said. Was it possible that the dragon had really winked? The borders between reality and her own wacky visions were becoming blurred. She certainly wasn't in Guyana any more.

Dear Felix,
Sorry I didn't get a chance to answer your last email. Internet cafés are not as easy to find here as they are in France. Too bad you don't like your new teacher. Don't be a botheration or you'll live to regret it.

As for me, there's so much happening I don't know where to begin. Now, a few of these details might make Mom and Dad a little nervous, so spare them the fretting, will you? Tell them I'm fine, safe, healthy, and having the time of my life.

I've been thinking a lot about you, since one of the people I've been travelling with reminds me of you. He has some of your mannerisms, and the same intensity. Strangely enough, the other person I'm travelling with reminds me of Mom. It's bizarre that even the strange things are familiar.

I am on a train, leaving Beijing and heading towards Nanjing and eventually Shanghai. The days we spent in Beijing were interesting, magical, and even spooky. After visiting the Forbidden City, where my friend Christopher swore he saw a marble dragon wink at him, we did more sightseeing and went out to a restaurant in the BeiHei Park, a beautiful park with a small lake in the middle of it. Your favourite hero, Kublai Khan, built his palace there, where Marco Polo was said to have visited him. Along the lake is a wall with a ceramic mosaic of nine dragons that sport giant pearls.

The restaurant was also really something. After our appetisers, Christopher was still going on about the dragons and the fact that he was communing with them, when the waiter brought us our second course. Arghh! Even mentioning it again makes me sick to my stomach. You'll never believe this, but it was SNAKE! I yelped and the waiter took it away. The manager came to our table to explain that it was a delicacy, but not for the life of me was I having any of that. I settled for some beef (at least I hope it was beef) in a kind of orange sauce.

The next day we went in a tour bus to the Great Wall. On the way we passed the valley of the Ming tombs, where the Emperors are buried. The bus stopped to let us out to examine the tombs, and we walked through the archways towards the Avenue of the Animals, a long pathway lined with stone statues of lions, monkeys, oxen, snakes, and, of course, dragons.

This time it was Sean who became a bit batty. He was gazing at one of the monkey statues, when all of a sudden he yelped: "Ouch! Stop that!" and turned around to brush something off his bottom. He turned around to find no one and nothing there. Christopher couldn't stop laughing, and I joined him. Sean looked frightened, as if he'd been attacked or bitten. When we asked him to explain what happened, he said, "You're never going to believe this…" and he kept shaking his head, the way he had that day on the ridge after his fall. His scar seemed to be throbbing; his blue eyes sparkled. He took a deep breath before continuing,

"It felt like the monkey came from the statue and pulled on what felt like MY tail!" He was serious, but when we burst out laughing again his face brightened, and he started to giggle.

The oddness of China was beginning to feel normal. Later, Christopher said he was certain that one of the stone dragons had been watching him. Things were really becoming like a movie, and I had to accept that there had been something magical about the day.

Back on the bus, we travelled past men on donkey carts that reminded me of Mister Tims. Remember the bandy-legged old man who rode his donkey cart through Georgetown? But in Beijing there were many carts and many more bicycles, also carrying cargo.

At the Great Wall I was awestruck. It seemed to go on forever. The walk is hilly, over stones, and it's a long trek towards the towers. When we finally got to the far tower, I was out of breath, and my feet were sore.

The three of us were examining the height of the wall. Christopher was showing me some markings on a brick, while Sean moved on slightly ahead of us. He stood staring back along the wall's great expanse. From the other side of the footpath, a woman was taking photographs. Suddenly I recognised her with a shock – the short American woman with wild, curly red hair. The same woman I'd run my cart into at Heathrow and who had chased an Arab boy through the market in Paris. This seemed too much of a coincidence, but, as I had begun to believe, anything was possible. The woman walked towards Sean.

"Could you please move. You're blocking my view," she blurted out rather rudely.

Sean looked at her, not understanding what she was talking about, given the miles of wall to his left and right. The woman had her camera raised, and I guess she was trying to take a picture of the section of wall behind Sean.

"Is there something in particular you'd like to photograph here?" Sean asked politely.

The woman lowered her camera and looked carefully at Sean before she spoke.

"I honestly don't think it's any of your business what I want to photograph," she said, trying to be polite, but not succeeding.

"It's just that I don't understand why you want me to move," continued Sean, staring hard at the woman's face, getting annoyed.

"Well, that's not the point, is it, whether you understand or not. I asked you to move and now I expect that you will…" she said harshly.

"Bit of a witch, isn't she," whispered Christopher into my ear, careful not to be overheard by the woman, who was a few feet away.

"You'd better believe it. It's the same woman we saw in Paris, with the stolen wallet, remember?" I said to Christopher. He nodded in recognition.

Sean gave the woman a stern look, and they held each other's stare as though in a showdown. But suddenly the woman turned to look at something that had caught her attention. Christopher was juggling. He had taken out some small balls from his bag and was tossing them up, and they were magically circling one another in the air.

His attempt to distract them had worked. When the woman's eyes fell on Christopher, she appeared to soften, her face getting brighter, her eyes glistening, enjoying what they were seeing.

"Well, hello," she said in a sweet voice as she moved towards him.

Christopher didn't take his eyes off the balls, but said "Hello."

He was having a strong effect on the woman. She watched him with delight.

"You're fantastic!… and also very cute…" she exclaimed. "Would you have a drink with me?"

"Um…" Christopher took a split-second glance towards Sean and me, while we both stood silently, amazed at what we were hearing. Could this woman be the one of Christopher's dreams? I could hardly imagine it.

"Well, actually, no, I don't think so…" he said finally, keeping the balls circling in the air.

"Oh, come on, don't be shy…" she said forcefully.

"Really, no, I couldn't…" he said.

"Why not?"

"Well…" he hesitated, glanced quickly at us again then focussed again on the balls. He took a few seconds to muster some strength. "…I don't think we're really well suited."

"Oh!" the woman said, offended. "Oh, not your type… not good enough, eh? Oh… you…" and her voice broke off, and I could feel her anger growing as she searched for the right words.

"You… gypsy ditsy little faggot!" she yelled finally.

One ascending ball hit another coming down and ricocheted off it in the opposite direction, hitting the wall, while the other two balls bounced to the ground and rolled down the footpath. Christopher stood with his arms at his sides, in horror at the woman's words. I'd never seen him drop anything before. He has always been an expert juggler. Sean moved towards the woman with his fist curled, and I thought the whole thing was going to break into a brawl, but I pulled them both away by the sleeves of their shirts, begging them to ignore her. She walked away in a huff, and we walked in the opposite direction. By the time we got back into the bus we were exhausted, and as the bus headed back to the city we were all relieved.

"Now that's just too much of a coincidence," I said as I stared out of the window.

Christopher smiled and took a photograph of me. "There are no coincidences, as I learned in the circus, there are only inevitabilities," he said.

"She was hot on ya, mate," Sean teased. "Maybe you should've given her a chance, you never know, the woman of a man's dreams may come disguised…!"

"Not on your life," Christopher said, shaking his head. He put his headset on to listen to music. Sean smiled, then his face grew serious. He shook his head and looked fierce, on the verge of a roar.

"He's right, actually. I know faces," he said, "and that one is troubled. And she causes trouble…" He looked into his lap and shook his head again. I began to have a very eerie feeling about all of this and hoped that it was just another one of China's little magic tricks.

Well, little brother, I wanted to keep you up-to-date on the trip and the crazy things you'd like. It's been the most interesting time of my life, and I'm not sure how I'm ever going to feel right about being home again, even though some days I'm so homesick I can barely stand it! I hope you're taking good care of Mom and Dad. Tell them I send them a big hello and lots of love, and, remember, don't tell them these details. I don't want them fretting and asking me to phone home every day. As it is, calling is hard enough on the days we planned. You take good care of yourself.

Your travelling sister,
Bea

Nanjing, China

Mesmerised by the landscape lumbering by on the other side of the glass, Beatrice stared out of the train window. Next to her, Christopher was dozing with his headphones on. Sean was walking the length of the train, visiting each of the cars to see who and what they contained. China was having the same effect on all of them. It was magical, with so much to discover, so much hidden under the surface, all of it ancient. Beatrice's visions had become wilder. Everywhere she looked she saw bizarre images that in Georgetown she would have attributed to her wild imagination. Here they were real, and she was starring in her own adventure movie.

The train wound through miles and miles of grassy hills, river valleys and rice fields, where farmers bent low in their labour. Beasts of burden dragged huge wooden ploughs. Beatrice wondered what her connection to these people was. Where had her great-great-great grandfather grown up? What had he done other than cultivate rice? What if he had never left China? Would she have grown up bending over wet grass tending these fields?

Sean returned with a wicked smile on his face.

"You'll never guess who I ran into in the next car up," he said with some zeal.

"Who?" Beatrice asked.

"The American woman we saw at the Great Wall. Remember? That witch..."

"Oh, no!" Beatrice gasped. She nudged Christopher to wake him up. He took off his headset and wiped a spot of sleep drool from his cheek.

"It's true," Sean continued, and his railway-track scar became prominent again, "and she's as witchy as ever. She asked me if I was English, having heard an accent that she couldn't place. English! She's an ignorant bitch! I went to prison because of someone with a face as wretched as hers."

Beatrice could feel a tingle of fear along her shoulders. Why was the American woman reappearing? What would she be like now that Christopher had rejected her? She didn't seem to take rejection lightly. Beatrice had known others like her. People who felt hard-done by no matter what their situation was. And now both she and Christopher had somehow offended her. Was she out to make trouble for them?

"Maybe she fancies *you*, Sean," Beatrice said, trying to ignore the fear.

"Arghh! Please, the woman is wretched. I bet she's following us. Or maybe she's been sent to follow me..." he said, suddenly terrified and looking about the compartment.

"Not possible, Sean," Christopher added quickly.

"I asked her where she was going," Sean continued. "She spewed some silly business-speak answer about being on a world-wide journey. Some company that wants to make millions making fast food or some such shite..."

"Actually, not fast food. Better food, you moron," said a voice behind Sean, cutting him off. Christopher and Beatrice looked behind Sean to see the woman in the aisle, her flaming red hair framing her face. Sean turned around quickly.

"Now, look here..." he said. Beatrice sensed his anger rising. His leonine eyes started to bulge and his hands were slowly forming into fists. The woman barely noticed and continued to rail at them.

"Don't tell me... let me guess... you three are doing that searching for yourself thing that all spoiled brats around the world do, right?"

"Excuse me?" said Christopher, more than a little put off.

"You know ... can't stand to stay at home, parents bug you, they're telling you what to do and then they give you some money to keep you quiet. So you strap on a backpack to look like adventurers and," she snapped her fingers, "*voilà*... instant adventure."

The three of them stared in disbelief at this horrible woman. Beatrice thought of what her Auntie Mavis would say to the woman: "Girl, you have the class of a saltfish..." and then she'd suck her teeth and turn on her heels to walk away. Auntie Mavis could tolerate neither rudeness nor arrogance. And she would have resented the idea that her money had come easily and that Beatrice was spoiled. Christopher had run away to the circus and then away from the circus. Sean had spent a few years in jail. Hardly spoiled rich kids. Perhaps the woman was talking about herself without knowing it. She was fidgety and nervous, shuddering ever so slightly now and then, as though battling with herself inside.

"Look, Miss," Beatrice said politely. "We have nothing against you, so why have you come to insult us like this?"

The young woman looked hard at Beatrice, up and down, stopping for a few seconds at her red shoes. Then she looked her in the eye. "Oh, very exotic, aren't we? And what are you, young thing?"

A prickly anger burned in Beatrice's cheeks.

"What kind of question is that?" she asked, biting her tongue to stop from being more rude.

"You know, what are you? Chinese, Polynesian, Mexican? You look a little exotic to me…"

There it was again, that question, and this time from one of the most unpleasant women Beatrice had ever met.

"Guyanese, if you have to know," Beatrice answered, her eyes glaring, her blood boiling.

"That's not a race, that's a nationality, you dimwit," the woman answered back, sounding like a know-it-all. The woman looked at Christopher with a hurt scowl. He smiled at her, trying to make her feel better, but her scowl became even more intense. Suddenly he leaned across Beatrice from his seat and swept his hands behind the woman's ear. A plastic flower materialised in his hand.

"No hard feelings?" he asked, with a smile holding the flower up to her. The woman became flustered. She felt her ear, her face, and in embarrassment she turned on her heels and left. Sean moved his foot into the aisle just enough to have her stumble over it.

"You good-for-nothing idiots, you…" she murmured as she caught herself from falling. She straightened up and headed quickly back to the next compartment.

Christopher couldn't help but giggle when she was out of earshot. "Sean, you're terrible, and if it had been anyone else I'd be cross with you now, but she is the most hideous woman I've ever met!"

"Where on earth did you get that flower, mate?" asked Sean.

"Ah, that's magic..." Christopher answered with a smile.

Beatrice was trembling. The fear she felt at the woman's reappearance had intensified, and although her friends made light of it, she could tell they felt the tension the woman had brought with her. Beatrice tried to relax; she stared out of the window.

The train reached Nanjing. The three companions had planned to disembark, to visit the Purple and Gold Mountains, but they stood back, away from the doors, while Sean kept watch at the window to see if the American woman would alight at that station. They agreed that if she were going to Nanjing they would continue on the train towards Shanghai, avoiding another encounter. Sean saw her on the platform and motioned to the others to go back to their seats.

The train chugged off peacefully southward, the temperature getting hotter by the mile. It followed alongside a huge muddy river, passing miles and miles of rice fields. When it stopped at Suzhou, just outside of Shanghai, the three friends decided to get off to visit this small town that reminded Christopher of Venice, Italy.

Shanghai, China

WWW.WORLDMAIL.COM

> Dear Mom and Dad

> I've finally found somewhere to write email.

> China feels suspended in time. Except Shanghai, which is a
> booming place with endless construction, traffic jams of posh
> cars, and pavements crammed with people on their way to
> work, speaking on their cell phones. What a contrast to the
> rural areas.

> We stopped in Suzhou on the way here. Suzhou is called the
> Venice of the East because of its canals and the fact that most
> of the daily life takes place on the waterway. The name of the
> town means Plentiful Water. Well it's plentiful lush too!
> Gardens and silk! It's famous for silk production. I have
> bought myself a silk dress to go with the red shoes I bought in
> London. Now I really do look like Suzy Wong, the way you all
> used to tease me when I was a child. Don't worry, I haven't
> taken up her profession.

> Something about Suzhou was comforting. The boats, the
> water and the simple life – it's amazing to think that I might
> have a distant relation as far away and exotic as China. I
> suppose it's possible that we are related to someone in just
> about any place on earth.

> Suzhou is not a big city, yet it still felt crowded. But nothing
> compares to Shanghai. The friends I've met along the way
> have come with me here. Of all the places we've been so far,

73

> Shanghai is the most overwhelming to us. The food sold in the
> snack stalls is tasty, but bizarre. Do you know that they eat
> snakes, pangolin (a kind of scaly anteater), monkey and dog
> here? Luckily for me they also eat lobster and prawns, my
> favourite. My friend Christopher knows a lot about Chinese
> food, and he directs us to the really good treats, which I
> never would have dared to try. I am eating a lot. We walk and
> walk and perspire and talk, and sometimes I fret about what
> on earth Auntie Mavis wanted me to see, but here I am.

> And it's hot. The farther south we go, the hotter it gets. Hong
> Kong will be like Georgetown in August. Christopher has
> family there. He's looking for the woman of his dreams and
> thinks she might be in Hong Kong after all, like his parents
> have always told him.

> Well, Mom and Dad, I miss you a lot. This trip has really been
> something. The months are passing so quickly. In some ways
> it seems like years and in other ways merely days. The
> world is a fascinating place. I wish Auntie Mavis could see me
> now!

> Love always, Your daughter, Beatrice

October 14

Diary, the strangeness continues. Since we arrived in China the supernatural has taken over. We are in Shanghai, a city of 14 million people and sprawling over far more square miles than Los Angeles, and yet who do we meet as we're strolling along the Huangpu River in the centre of the city? None other than the horrible woman herself. Her name is Cynthia Buckley, oddly enough the same surname as my wretched teacher at Bishop's. That's one strange thing, but there are more. When Cynthia saw us, she approached us and was sweet-talking. So sweet we could hardly believe she was the same person who'd been so rude at every other encounter. She told us about the work she is doing in major centres around the world, in her position as the director of marketing and research for an international biotechnology firm. She boasted about being the youngest department director the company has ever had (she's 23), and she's been sent on a world research and development mission. The company is trying to build a reputation in developing countries, where most of their research is conducted. "Bio-engineering is the future!" she exclaimed. According to Cynthia, her company wants to "engineer the world," which she said with a bit too much zeal for my comfort. She has a bit of a sneer, even when she's trying to look friendly. Her face gives me the shivers. I don't trust her.

Cynthia invited us to dine that evening at a special restaurant in an area called the Bund. The Bund was once off limits to "dogs and Chinese" - in that order - during the time before the Cultural Revolution when foreigners and social climbers limed about, taking themselves very seriously. It was a place where musicians, artists and writers, mostly from Britain, gathered to get away from the rest of the city. The three of us were hesitant to accept, but she was convincing and offered a limousine to pick us up at our hotel, so we agreed. Sean was the most suspicious. His paranoia got the better of him, and Cynthia's re-appearances seemed a little too coincidental. "They're out to get me, I know, I know…" he said shaking his head. Christopher and I had never asked him exactly who "they" were, and we didn't start now. Christopher's curiosity had been pricked by Cynthia's invitation to such a famous area, and he felt more comfortable with her now, since it seemed she had stopped fancying him.

"Come on, we could have a laugh," he said and then took a coin out from behind Sean's ear. "And I'll buy…" he added.

Sean smiled, and we both followed Christopher down the road.

A row of waiters and cooks greeted us at the restaurant. We were the only foreigners in the room, it seemed, the others looking like regular Shanghai restaurant guests. We were seated at a very elegant table. I saw Cynthia at another table, talking intensely with a group of clients. I overheard her mention her father's business, which apparently he lost a few years ago, for some reason I couldn't make out. Whatever happened to him seemed to make Cynthia riled up. Her face became flushed as she spoke about it to a Chinese man at her table. "They were wrong, I know they were. He'd never do anything like that..." she said, "and now I'm left holding the bag, forced on my own. Daddy never takes that into account..." she added bitterly, and then quickly got up from the table.

She came over to our table, all smiles and politeness - that woman is a two-faced harpy! She told us we could order anything we wanted and that she was going to pick up the tab. We looked at each other warily, but when we examined the menu we finally understood. This was a restaurant that served weird dishes like geep (a cross between goat and sheep), broccleflower (a broccoli and cauliflower blend) and other engineered plants and animals that were explained on the menu: things like roasted tomatoes with pigskin that made for a juicy, porky gravy! I was never so disgusted in my life. I felt like I was in Frankenstein's workshop. This was not just genetic modification, this was a whole darker side of what Cynthia and her company thought they could achieve to make money. Further down on the menu there was a description of farm-grown beefette - beef from cattle that had been bred with genes to make them smaller so that they took up less space in a field and so farmers could have more of them. The image of bonsai trees jumped to mind. Bonsai beef! And there was another description under "Cynthia's Special" that read: "Marinated tri-drumsticks - a delicious roasted dish made from our new, more efficient three-legged chickens." Apparently since drumsticks are so popular, they want to give people more of them in one chicken. My stomach turned. Were we her guinea pigs? Now I understood why she'd been so nice to us. She was using us to test her company's experiments in new cuisine.

Christopher decided on vegetables - in the best sauces of a fine Chinese restaurant - but Sean wanted to be more daring, so he ordered the geep, which he said was tasty and very tender. I couldn't bring myself to eat anything. I stuck with water. Even that I sipped cautiously. When Cynthia came to our table and saw that I wasn't eating, she lost her polite act and started yelling at me:

"Well, you'd think you'd try something, seeing that it's free and all. ... I should have figured. You're those precious types, can't take anything just a little daring or unusual. We're on the cusp of a whole new industry here! You're looking at the state of the art in agriculture; you're looking at the future, you morons! And to think I considered letting you and your rich daddies in on an investment.

Stock prices are going to be higher than your grandmother at Christmas by the time you losers wake up and smell the coffee. And this was even going to be my treat! You ungrateful little..." but she broke off, turned on her heels and headed into the kitchen.

"I want to get out of here," I said to Christopher and Sean.

They agreed and didn't finish their meals. Out in front of the restaurant we noticed a small black dog with short, shiny fur lying on the pavement, licking its paws with great delight. I bent down to pat the poor thing, which I thought must be hungry, teased by the smell of all that food wafting from the restaurant.

Now diary, this is where it gets spooky. When I touched the dog's head, it looked up at me. I screamed and pulled my hand away. I swear to you now, my dear, dear diary, that the thing had the face of baboon. I know no one is ever going to believe me, but I swear it is true. I ran down the street away from the restaurant. Christopher and Sean followed me, calling out and asking what was wrong. I had to catch my breath at a corner just before the end of the Bund district. They caught up with me and quizzed me on my scream and sudden flight. I told them what I had seen, but they both looked at each other in disbelief. They knew that funny things were happening to us all - Christopher and his dragons, Sean with the monkey pulling his phantom tail - but I don't think either of them could fathom what I'm sure I saw. It seemed too bizarre to possibly be true. Christopher patted me on the shoulder and took a bouquet of flowers from behind my back and offered them to me. I still don't know how he does that.

Hong Kong, China

Beatrice, Sean, and Christopher were slurping noodles from bowls as they stood at the counter of a noodle vendor in a street near the Hong Kong harbour. It was mid-morning. After their long train and coach ride the previous day they had arrived in Hong Kong and checked into a youth hostel. Overwhelmed by the restaurants to choose from, they had picked one that offered the strangest delicacies, from dog to eel, and again Beatrice felt unable to indulge in the delicacies and simply ordered two bowls of rice, which satisfied her for the night.

Now she was famished, and gulped down the delicious noodle soup. The loud slurping and sucking noises from the three travellers took the place of conversation. Beatrice swallowed some warm broth, then raised her eyes towards the boats. A stew of freighters, tugs, hydrofoils, junks, ferries, sampans, and yachts jostled in the harbour. Her camera eye zoomed in on one of the junks. She felt herself tossed slowly in the wake of the other boats on the harbour as she prepared the sails and ropes of her vessel. Suddenly the wind picked up. She was in a storm, the junk tossing about on the sea. Ahead there were other ships. Pirate ships. There was a battle going on for silk, for spices, and she was caught in the middle. Her part called for her to scream, so she let out a violent cry and kept tapping the heels of her red shoes together: "Help! They've captured me! Help!"

"Who's captured you?" Sean said urgently, terrified by the call for help. He held Beatrice's two arms; the noodles from her bowl now spilled all over the front of her shirt. She snapped back into the present.

"Oh, sorry... I was just... I mean, just sort of a daymare. You know, nightmare/daymare... happens very rarely," she assured them. Her inability to control her fantasies was beginning to worry her, but perhaps it was a sign of how free her imagination was becoming.

Sean and Christopher finished their soup, watching her warily. Beatrice tried not to show her embarrassment. What was the treasure Auntie Mavis had promised? Was it money? Was it fame? She was finding the notion of fame harder and harder to imagine. She was already being accepted for who she really was, and had come across strange magic and met unusual people. She had thought that all the people around the world would be so different from her, but they seemed not so different at all.

All the people except Cynthia Buckley, of course, who seemed unreasonably nasty and unhappy. Beatrice tried to feel sorry for her, knowing what Auntie Mavis said: "Everybody loses goodness from time to time, but some forget where to look for it… and dey never find it again…" Cynthia seemed to be one of those who didn't know where to look. Or maybe she was part of her company's own experiments, a kind of genetically engineered employee, all head and no heart. Perhaps crossbred with a bull or a lizard.

After their soup, the three friends walked through the crowded streets, amid skyscrapers and double-deck trams and buses. Six million people were crammed into this tiny enclave called the "fragrant harbour." Fragrant indeed, thought Beatrice, but not flowery, more like the smell of diesel and spices mixed together. Her first sight of Hong Kong's skyline had taken her breath away. She'd never seen such a packed city. As they walked along the street now, she was longing for Georgetown and the scent of the sea while standing at the seawall.

Sean stopped and stood by a sign that said Aberdeen, which they'd heard was Hong Kong's oldest settlement. Aberdeen was a floating town, where people lived their entire lives on junks and sampans in the harbour.

"There's still so much of Britain in this place," said Sean, shaking his head.

"And so much of China," Christopher added, pointing to a wobbly rickshaw as old as its driver. Suddenly Sean was running beside the rickshaw driver and motioning to him. The man didn't understand what Sean wanted and kept running. Sean grabbed the rickshaw's handles and started pulling it, much to the man's dismay and with many protestations from him. Sean and the man disappeared into the traffic, while Christopher and Beatrice watched them.

"What on earth is he doing?" Christopher asked.

"I have no idea," Beatrice answered. They sat down on the curb and waited for their friend to return. Christopher looked distracted. He took out some tiny balls and started to juggle them.

"What's the matter?" Beatrice asked.

"Oh, I was just thinking of those dragons on the mainland. I think they were a sign."

"A sign of what," she asked, still uneasy remembering the sight of the baboon-faced dog.

"A sign that things are not always as we see them, and that means for me that maybe I've been looking for love down the wrong path," he concluded sadly, and let the balls drop.

"Maybe you're looking too hard. It could take a lifetime to find love, I think. And maybe it starts with yourself."

Beatrice was surprised at her own words. She had no idea where they came from or how she knew what she felt she knew. But at that moment she was sure of what she was saying and felt very wise. Maybe this trip was showing her something after all.

When Sean returned he told them he had wanted to relieve the man's burden and to get a little exercise, so he took the rickshaw with its customer to their destination and ran back. The man thanked him and thanked him, and Sean felt he'd done a kind deed. He felt less paranoid about being followed. The three of them boarded a bus that took them to Aberdeen, the floating community.

They arrived to the colours and sounds of the floating life and immediately stood in a queue for a boat taxi to take them on a tour. In front of them was a very small human creature, a boy with an old man's face. He was thin and gangly, looking childlike and yet grown up at the same time. Sean peered over his shoulder.

"He's reading Aristotle!" Sean whispered to Beatrice. "I read that in prison. It's not an easy read," he said, shaking his head and drifting off into the past for a moment. He took a step forward towards the boy.

"I thought what he said about the golden mean was interesting," Sean said to him. Beatrice was impressed by Sean's ability to talk about such an obscure topic.

"Oh, I suppose so, maybe I'm not that far along yet, I'm trying, struggling, you see... ah, this is my first attempt... ah, never really read anything like this before... ah, you see I forget what I read all the time, yea, it's not so easy for me, I don't have the facility you see..." the young man mumbled and bumbled his way through his explanation. Looking up, the boy seemed even smaller. He barely reached Sean's underarm, and Sean was not a tall person. But the boy had the look of a wise man. His face was wrinkled and ropy. And his hair was thick and matted like straw.

"Well, don't worry," Sean said to the boy, trying to reassure him. "It's one of the most difficult things I've ever read. Maybe you should start with something more simple."

"Ah, yea, you're probably right, yes, well, thanks for the advice, oh, I am daft, aren't I? Always trying to do more than I can, at least that's what my Dad always tells me. He doesn't like books himself, says they corrupt the mind and lead people to unhappiness. I don't know, I don't know... I've always liked them, but he, well, he didn't really want us to read them, and now I feel I have so much to catch up on, you know? There are so many things to know and sometimes I don't feel I have the brain for it, or at least the memory. I like to read but then I think I forget so much, get carried away... oh, sorry, I'm rambling on, you didn't ask for that did you? Sorry, I'll be quiet now; you have a nice trip. Would you like to go ahead of me? I can't really remember why I chose to go on a tour anyway. I've been here for five days and seen just about all I want to see, but, well... you go ahead," he said and moved aside to let Sean, Beatrice and Christopher go ahead of him.

"That's very kind of you," said Beatrice, "but are you sure you don't want to go on the tour? Or maybe you'd like to join us? My name is Beatrice. This is Sean, and this is Christopher." She felt warm towards this man-child, and felt she'd known him before. In fact, there was something like her father in him, his kind awkwardness. He was so endearing, and yet, in contrast to her father, was unsure of himself. She had the urge to protect him.

"Oh, I couldn't impose, no, really. Really? Would that be okay with you? I mean I've barely talked to anyone these last few days and I think I've forgotten what it's like. Would you mind?"

"Of course not," Christopher said warmly. Beatrice could tell that the other two had also taken to this young man. Silently agreeing, they were accepting a new companion.

During the water-taxi tour of Aberdeen, the boy introduced himself as Deepak. He told them he was seventeen years old.

"People can never tell how old I am," he said quickly, "so I always have to tell them and they're often shocked, just like you are, I can see you're shocked, and I guess it's that I have rather an old face but a young body, a mix-up of nature I suppose, well..."

Deepak was taking some time away from his studies in order to travel. He lived in London but had been to school in San Francisco. His family was originally from India, where he'd never been, and he was slowly making his way there to see some of his mother's relatives in Delhi.

"You know people are very wise in India, very wise, and I've always thought I could learn something from them that I couldn't in California, you know, in California everything comes very quickly but I'm not sure if it sticks, if you know what I mean... it's just that in India they have a tradition of knowing things, knowing them from the inside out, if you know what I mean, or at least that's what my mother tells me. She doesn't mind that I read so much, it's only my Dad who does..."

California! thought Beatrice. Deepak had lived in California. Her dream! She had finally met someone who could tell her about the place, who could tell her whether she really could make a go of it there or not. She touched her tongue to her top lip and then ran it over the breadth of both lips. Her Judy Garland lips, as Stephanie called them. But there was a disturbing inkling in her that said she didn't feel like a movie star any more.

"What's it like to live in California?" she asked Deepak as the water-taxi pulled around a huge junk with a wide, bright red sail.

"Oh, California? Well, I guess you could say it's fine, yes, fine, good weather, well, sunny weather most of the time except in San Francisco, where it rains a bit, and fog, oh, boy that fog...

and well, I went to school there for a year, just a preliminary year, you see, just to make up for some of the courses I didn't take in London. And my Mom, well my Mom wants me to go to university there, but, my Dad, he isn't really up for it, wants me to join him in business in London. There are good universities in San Francisco, very good, I think, at least I think I'm going to go to one, if I can get in, if I get a scholarship, but, you know, I'm not sure whether I'll get one or not..."

"You tell your Dad you want to study," said Christopher, understanding the father–son pressure that Deepak described.

"Have you ever been to Hollywood?" Beatrice asked.

"Oh, well, yes, well, that's different. Nope, not a place for me. Nope..." and he shook his head.

Beatrice's heart sank. It wasn't what she was hoping to hear. She decided to ask no further questions, for fear of having more of the dream shattered. Somehow the fact that this very sweet young man was saying something negative about the place she'd always wanted to go made her uncomfortable. What was there left to hold on to of her old dream? This trip was dissolving it.

As they headed back in the water-taxi, Christopher invited Deepak to join them for dinner at his uncle's restaurant. Deepak was happy for the company. They dined on wonton soup, egg rolls, fried rice, chicken chow mein, and sweet and sour chicken with hearty appetites. After the meal, Christopher began to talk with his cousin's best friend, a girl with long hair to her waist. Beatrice noticed him blush and wondered if this was a sign of his affection for her. Later, when Beatrice teased him about it, Christopher smiled. He told her that he liked the sparkle in the girl's eyes, but that when they had spoken he realised they had nothing in common.

"Love is not just about looks," he concluded with a shrug. "Nope, Beatrice," he continued as they were leaving the restaurant, "still on the search."

Outside the restaurant they were reluctant to leave their new friend Deepak, who had continued to talk a mile a minute and to stutter and mumble through everything he said. Beatrice had become fond of his funny aged-looking face and his troll-like appearance. She realised that it was his old face, in folds like an elephant's hide, which reminded her of her father. Deepak had charmed them with stories of life in San Francisco as well as of his family in London. Sean and Christopher suggested that they all meet up when they got back to London. They were about to take their leave of each other when Deepak ran his hand through his matted hair and said suddenly:

'But, of course, why didn't I think of this earlier, oh stupid me, not thinking at all when I should. Of course, it would be perfect. Why don't you come with me to India? To Delhi, and of course you must see some of the rest, but you could stay with me at my aunt's house in Delhi and you could see a bit of the beauty of India. November is not a bad month in India, not too hot...What do you say? I mean I don't know much about it, and I can't say if you'll like it or not, but you'd be more than welcome, that is if you want to come, but maybe I'm talking out of turn here, maybe you don't want to come, but if you did that would be just fine with me and you'd have a place to stay... and...' The poor boy ran out of breath.

Beatrice, Christopher and Sean looked at each other, grinned and nodded. Without having to speak they knew that they agreed to follow this funny fellow to wherever he was going.

"We're in," said Beatrice, and she gave poor flabbergasted Deepak a pat on the shoulder.

Delhi, India

November 3

Dear Diary

Colour. Colour everywhere as though the world was a palette of paint, an array of brilliant shades, ready to be mixed up together. Red, yellow, and orange, all bright, with trim lined in gold to highlight the colours even more. The South Asian families at home have always been known for their colourful clothes, but here there is colour in the streets, on bicycles, hanging in windows and stalls, and in every home I've peeked into. Red is the most vibrant, and in my red shoes I do not feel like I stand out too much.

We are staying with Deepak's family near the centre of Delhi, very close to Connaught Place, where all the roads meet and their pattern creates an inner, middle, and outer circle lined with shops and restaurants. It's like a spiral maze. When we arrived yesterday I was bewildered and lost most of the day. Deepak's aunt is the complete opposite of her nephew. She is beautiful, tall and elegant. She has been very generous to us, offering us rooms and food, and taking us to see the sights of Delhi. I am still puzzled, diary, because I feel so comfortable in each odd place. I still don't know what the treasure is I'm to find, according to Auntie Mavis, but I'm yet another step closer.

I am travelling with the most remarkable friends, three young men who don't fit in where they've come from but are looking for themselves in the world. They are odd characters, all unique and even strange, but they are honest with themselves. Sometimes their honesty makes me ashamed. I think I wanted to be an actress so that I never had to be myself, so that I could cover up all the time and be things in my imagination rather than in the world. But I haven't been able to cover up at all. Everyone sees me and tells me I'm like them, or like someone they know. I am searching for more clues.

GREETINGS FROM DELHI

Dear Stephanie, I have made yet another
friend, but a very small one. He's young
but old at the same time. Indian, but has lived in California and
now lives in London. He wanted to come to India to gain the
ancient wisdom of his ancestors. He wants wisdom more than
anything else in the world. He says the funniest things, but he
doesn't know he's being funny. He lacks confidence – I think
partly because of his size – and thinks he's stupid, but he
doesn't seem so to me. We are all getting very close. We're all
out of place, but all searching, each for something different.
Sean wants courage; Christopher wants romance; and Deepak
wants wisdom. What do I want? In any case, around them I feel
safe. And we laugh quite a lot. Will write again soon,

Love, Beatrice

The smell of jasmine and chestnuts struck her as Beatrice
strolled through the grounds. She looked around for its source
but couldn't see anything obviously responsible for the alluring
odour. The cremation ground on the banks of the River Yamuna
is the final resting-place of national leaders of India, including
Nehru, and Indira and Rajiv Gandhi. Deepak had wanted to take
his new friends there because he had heard from his cousins that
being around the spirit of wise people helped bring wisdom.
They wandered about the cremation grounds and visited the
Mahatma Gandhi Museum, but Deepak felt restless. He decided
they should see the zoo, so they wandered over towards it and
Beatrice thought she could hear a faint roar coming from beyond
the gate. When they entered, they made their way to the cages
of huge white tigers. Staring at the magnificent beasts, Sean felt
something pull what seemed like a tail, but when he looked
back, there was nothing. Later, at the monkey compound,
Christopher looked straight into the eyes of a bearded white

primate, and then he too jumped, startled, and he swore to the others that it had said, "I love you." The monkey supposedly unfolded wings that had been tucked behind its front limbs and flew off out of the park. Beatrice and Sean laughed so hard they were almost not to be believed. They were all getting more concerned that these were not illusions at all. Something very peculiar was happening to them. When they asked Deepak whether or not he'd ever experienced any strange occurrences on his journey, he had to think a moment, then said, quite matter-of-factly, "Meeting you lot, that's all..."

His words seemed to calm them, and the four friends boarded a bus for another famous sight, just outside the city. As the coach left the cremation grounds, Deepak had a frown on his droopy, wrinkled face that made him look even older and stranger than before.

"I don't feel any different from when I arrived," he said sadly to Beatrice. She rubbed the top of his matted and stringy head. Her heart went out to him, because he seemed so determined to achieve magically something brilliant.

The bus turned onto the Mehruali-Badarpur road, and pulled into the fourteenth-century ruins of the Tughlaqabad Fort. They had decided to visit this ancient headquarters of the sultanate Tughlaq because, as Deepak had told them, the sultan had been an intellectual who was convinced of the force of reason along with creative ideas. During his reign there were fifteen different rebellions by those who thought that his attitude to governing was unrealistic. It was an eerie, deserted site, and the guidebook had warned specifically not to visit it alone. The group had wondered why, but they felt safe in each other's company.

Upon leaving the bus, Beatrice could sense in the air the fraught tension of ancient battles between the nobles and the Sultan. As they walked towards the ruins they suddenly heard behind them a thundering voice. "Arghh! So, we meet again!"

All four turned and, to their horror, saw Cynthia Buckley emerging from the main fort. Cynthia was accompanied by a group of tough-looking thugs dressed in traditional military attire, all in white, with red and yellow striped hats like a cross between turbans and top hats. Each of the five had a thick red belt from which hung a long sabre, sheathed in gold.

Beatrice, Sean and Christopher looked at one another and simultaneously nodded, turned, and headed rather quickly in the opposite direction. Sean pulled Deepak by the arm. Confused and dazed, Deepak mumbled to himself that he thought the woman was talking to them and maybe they were being rude to ignore her.

"Quiet," Sean said to him, under his breath, "she hates us and she'll hate you too..."

"Now wait just a minute!" came Cynthia's shrieking voice that rang out through the ruins. "You get back here this instant!" The four friends didn't stop, but suddenly before them stood two of her guards, towering over them like colossal statues, blocking their way.

"Where do you think you're going?" Cynthia called out from behind the thugs as she pulled something from her handbag. "I have a little something here that we should settle up right now! A little bill I think you must have forgotten, because I can't imagine that you'd be so ignorant as to think you could just get away with not paying for a meal and then leaving a country.... Who do you think you are, now really? You think life is free?"

Sean walked towards Cynthia with his eyes blazing with anger. He rolled up his sleeves.

"Look, you, you, little witch you..." he started, but Cynthia gasped and her guards moved a step closer to him. Sean stepped back. Christopher came to his side and was suddenly waving his arms and saying a spell of sorts. Beatrice thought she was imagining it, but she could swear she saw Cynthia levitate slightly off the ground before one of her guards pulled her back. Another guard moved forward and grabbed Christopher. He held his arms tightly behind his back, but Christopher didn't struggle.

"You were the one who invited us – coerced us into going!" Christopher said boldly.

"You wouldn't know coercion if it spat on you, you little hocus pocus mule... what the hell were you doing just then?" Cynthia asked, feeling herself to make sure she was all there. "And this little one..." she continued, pointing at Beatrice, "didn't even have the courtesy to eat anything at all! That's what I call rude and obnoxious."

"Look, you!" said Sean as he advanced, but he was blocked by a guard. Beatrice stepped up to Cynthia with as much calm as she could muster.

"Now, look here, since we met you, you've been nothing but rude and critical towards all of us. Then you sweet-talk us and invite us to your horrible restaurant and have the nerve…"

"Horrible? How dare you? You wouldn't know horrible if it bit you on the ankle!"

"Well, I mean, I don't know what it is you're trying to do…"

"Exactly, you don't, so why are you so quick to judge? I know your type… You're some bumpkin-Third-World-little-lost-missy looking for some place other than your own poverty-stricken country to cling to and then make all the rest of us look after you…"

"What would you dare claim to know about me?" Beatrice asked in a raised voice, cutting her off.

"I've travelled all my life, and my father dealt with your lot his whole life. I know all about it… When we were forced to leave…" and then she broke off, as though she'd said something she hadn't meant to. She looked back at the guards, one of whom was eyeing her very spitefully. She continued in a more hushed voice: "You and your little entourage of boys, well, let me tell you something, you should hightail it back to your pathetic corner of the world because you don't belong roaming around. You're not helping things any. Do you know what it costs to feed the world? Do you have any idea?"

Deepak cleared his throat and stepped forward. "Now, excuse me, uh, uh, I may not be correct about this, but well, uh, as far as I understand it, there's plenty of food to feed the world, it's just that it's wasted and not distributed, and as far as criticising my friends here, it would seem to me, uh, but I may be wrong, yes, but it would seem to me, by my calculations, and excuse me for saying so, that they don't owe you money for something they didn't ask…"

"Now, who have we got here?" Cynthia interrupted. "Another little exotic friend for our charming girl with the red shoes? This one looks like a little toad. Don't they feed you at home kid? Where on earth did you come from and what could you possibly know? And what right do you have to be talking to me in the first place?"

"I have every right, as far as I can tell, and don't call me any names. I'm not afraid of you," defended Deepak bravely.

"Oh, you should be, though, you stupid wart-bred-troll. You know nothing and don't try to use any rhetoric you read in bleeding-heart magazines on me. We're making business here, plain and simple. And business helps everyone," Cynthia concluded.

Just then Deepak took a huge step towards her, where he came barely up to her chest. He grabbed the restaurant bill she had been waving at them, and tore it out of her hands. He held it up to her face and ripped it to shreds right before her eyes. Both guards made a move for him, releasing Christopher and Sean, but Deepak ducked under their arms and was behind them in no time.

"Why you little..." she began, but Deepak whispered, "Let's get out of here," and the four ran in the direction of the main fort. Deepak's size didn't help his speed. Very soon one of the guards caught up with him, grabbed him by the shirt and detained him. The others kept running but stopped and hid behind a fort wall. They watched their friend being interrogated by the guards.

"What should we do? Should we go and get him?" asked Christopher, breathless and worried.

"Um, yes, I guess I should go," said Sean, straightening his shirt and taking a deep breath.

"No, look," said Beatrice. "They're letting him go. They probably only wanted to frighten him. He had nothing to do with the restaurant bill."

"Except for tearing it up," Christopher reminded her.

When Deepak reached them at the fort wall, he was calm and told them what the guards had said. Apparently he had reasoned with them in their language. They had no legal right to detain him. They let him go but told him they were going to keep an eye on the four of them. The slightest wrong move would have them all back in the hands of the guards, for questioning.

The friends sat at the bus stop waiting for the next coach to take them back to Delhi. Beatrice was seething with anger. Something about Cynthia really irked her, and, tempted as she was to teach her a lesson for her rudeness, Beatrice also thought it wise to keep clear of the woman. She felt protective of her friends. They were not only kind and enjoyable company, but they had strong principles. They coped with every new situation and acted with integrity. They were not born actors the way she was, trying to escape reality when it proved difficult. She admired them and wanted to be more like them.

Gujarat, India

WWW.WORLDMAIL.COM

> Dear Felix

> Thanks for your emails. Sorry I haven't been able to respond
> before now; it's not easy finding Internet access here. Glad to
> hear that school is better for you. But why aren't you playing
> cricket this year?

> The bizarre sights of this journey continue. We arrived in the
> south of India after some very strange days in Delhi. We
> encountered that horrible woman again. And later that night
> we took a rickshaw ride home from a man who told us he had
> been an ox in his last life and was very comfortable hauling
> the four of us in his vehicle. The thing is, my dear brother,
> he wasn't joking; he was quite serious and opened his mouth
> to show us his rather huge teeth, as though that would prove
> it. That was strange enough, but just after we arrived at
> Deepak's house I heard a continuous buzzing like the sound of
> a dozen flies. I asked the others if they could hear it, but none
> of them could. When we got out of the rickshaw and were
> walking away, I turned to look back at the man and, Felix, I
> swear it, there were flies buzzing around what I was sure
> was the man's TAIL! And the tail was swishing them away. I
> know you think I've just lost my mind completely, but I am
> telling the truth about what I saw. That hocus pocus shite you
> and your friends go on about is starting to make sense to me.
> What could all this mean?

> We left Delhi, in an effort to get away from the wretched
> Cynthia, but also because I think all of us are tired of big
> cities. We've come south to Gujarat, which is close to
> Porbandar, the birthplace of Mahatma Gandhi, who is a hero
> for both Christopher and Deepak. Did you know that Gandhi's
> motto was "My life is my message"? How is that for
> somethin'! We visited his birthplace yesterday and toured the
> small home he was raised in. I think of anywhere Christopher
> and Deepak have been it was this humble place that inspired
> them the most. Even this town, for me, though, wasn't quiet
> enough. I am in desperate need of silence and space. We are
> heading to Kerala next. I can't wait to be dipping into the sea
> again. It has been too long.

> Felix, I know I bugged you, teased you, and complained all the
> time about you being a good-for-nothing, and a gangly mopey
> lie-about, but I want to let you know that I miss you. I'm
> going to be a better sister when I get back. I know you
> thought it was unfair of Auntie Mavis to leave me the money
> and unfair that I got to go on this trip, but I promise that
> you'll get to do something important one day soon. Like
> Christopher, I'm sure you'll do something interesting with all
> the passion you have firing you.

> For now, you stay well, and I'll write again soon.

> Love, Beatrice

Kerala, India

November 20

The sea, the sea, the sea! Ah, what bliss. Oh diary, I had no idea how starved I was for sun and a clear view to a distant horizon. It is magnificent here. We are almost at the tip of India, on the beach at Kovalam in rural Kerala. And today a professional masseur gave me a massage. I imagine movie stars get this kind of treatment every day, but for me it's special, and I'm feeling pampered and spoiled. I am writing this while drinking coconut milk. There is a scent of cardamom and cinnamon occasionally in the breeze. My three friends are with me. They are like family to me now, and I can't imagine a time when I didn't know them or feel connected to them in some very magical way.

We left Gujarat a week ago, and travelled again by train, choosing our destination at the last minute. Sean thought I might want to see Chennai (which used to be called Madras - famous, of course, for the fire-hot curries). Chennai is one of the filmmaking capitals of India, and that's saying a lot given that, as we were told, India makes more films than any other place in the world, including Hollywood.

We spent two days discovering Chennai, where the colours and clothing the women wear are more vibrant than anywhere else in India so far. Orange with purple, parrot-green with pink. Chennai is the centre of Tamil culture, and film is at its heart. "Nothing is impossible" is their motto: no plot too unrealistic, no stunt too difficult, no costume too daring. Sean pleaded with a producer, then charmed him into letting us onto the set of a historical movie with a bloody battle, elephants, men with arrows through their mouths, and even snakes! I despise snakes! It was fascinating for me to watch, since I'd never seen anyone making a film before. It's a long, slow process, and the actors do a lot of standing around. I think it might be even more fun to be behind the camera, the director. That's the person who makes it all happen. Maybe that's what I'd like to do.

Once again we were overwhelmed by people, so we decided to head for the beach. We booked a train to Kerala. And, diary, the strange coincidences on this trip have become almost ordinary. At the station, I heard a gentle voice behind me saying, "Somehow I knew we'd meet up again," and I turned around to see Linda, the beautiful flight attendant from my flight to London. She was dressed in long, white Indian trousers and flowing white blouse. She looked so beautiful that my spirits lit up at the sight of her.

"I can't believe it," I said, smiling.

"I can, we were destined to meet. You see, we have the same lines on our hands." She held up her palm to show it to me. She took my hand and opened the palm to the sky. With her index finger she traced a line across it, as though proving how much we were alike. Then she snapped her fingers, remembering something, and took a pen and paper out of her bag to jot it down.

I have to say that I was fascinated with her again. She is quirky but has a glowing power. Christopher couldn't keep his eyes off her. He stood staring at her as though she were the answer to all his dreams. She's almost twice his age, but her face is childlike, like a sprite's, and I can see why Christopher is infatuated with her.

She told us about her trip. She had taken time off work to come to India, to visit an ashram where she spent a week in silence and meditation. She was collecting herbs and spices that she uses at home in London to heal and treat ailments. She said she wanted to stop flying (that is, by airplane, she joked, and snapped her fingers again). She wants to open a practice in holistic living, where people from all over the world will come to share ideas, remedies for health and spirituality. Not to mention a few laughs, she added with a wink. "A city unto itself, a new way of life," she concluded.

"Human beings are essentially creative," she continued, "and we have to find a way to express creativity to its fullest." She adjusted some straps on her suitcase as we watched her, mesmerised. "I am hoping to go to Africa next, to bring home more secrets from there. Our lives began in Africa, you know." These words struck me as something from a dream, and then I remembered that Eddie and Richard had said almost exactly the same thing in London. I am really losing track of which things are in my imagination and which are real.

The four of us were speechless, in awe of Linda's beauty. It dawned on me that I would most certainly have to go to Africa too. I will suggest it to the others to see how they feel. It seems to me like an inevitable stop on this journey to what I must discover. Oh, Auntie Mavis, I feel your magic working somehow, perhaps through Linda, or just through my own steps along this road.

The travellers were hot, perspiring as they sat on the wooden seats of the waterbus that took them from the cashew-nut port and then down the grey-green canals of the Kerala backwaters. Beatrice examined Deepak's furrowed brow, as he was lost in thought. They had decided to visit this magical area of Kerala because Deepak had read about it in one of his favourite novels, *The God of Small Things.*

"Now there's a thinker," he had said of the book's author. "I'd like to think like that and to put all of those ideas and beautifully written images together in a book." And of course Deepak was indeed a small thing himself, and so must have felt great comfort in the book's message. Beatrice watched his feet dangling from his bench seat on the waterbus and wondered if he would ever grow. She felt certain he was not meant ever to be very big in stature, but perhaps big in thought. She touched his bony shoulder and he looked up at her with his piercing, pondering, dark eyes. He smiled and then looked out towards the shore. Beatrice caught sight of Christopher's glum face.

"Penny for your thoughts," she said to him quietly.

"All this beauty... all this beauty everywhere," he said quietly, with a slow tear staining his cheek. Beatrice touched her hand to his face. She understood how sentimental he was and had a surge of missing her brother.

The waterbus lurched, and she was shaken out of her mood. As the boat made its way through the tropical landscape lined with tidy picket-fenced gardens along the canal, a pair of crocodiles made their presence known beside the boat. Beatrice gasped.

"Oh my god, I've never seen one up close like that," she said as she caught her breath.

She sat back in her seat, but something about the sight felt ominous. She had trouble relaxing.

When they reached the bazaar, their tiny waterbus was heaved by the wake from a giant snakeboat powered by a hundred oarsmen. The chant of the oarsmen was low, like a rising hum as they rowed in training for a big race. The waterbus skirted the huge craft and docked. Stepping out of the boat and into the bazaar the friends were met by the sight of painted elephants, women with loads twice their weight on their heads, painted pots, vendors with fish, spices, coconut oils, and more elephants.

They browsed in the market, Sean leading them through the crowd as they took in the colours of spices and grains, and the smells of cooked food and incense. Suddenly the call of a painted elephant caught their attention. It was an unnatural, pained call. Sean stopped abruptly, causing Deepak to run into him, then Christopher to run into Deepak, and Beatrice to run into Christopher, like cars in a pile-up. The group came to a grinding halt.

"Oh, no," Sean said with terror in his voice. "Not possible."

None of the others could see what he was referring to. They turned to him with questioning faces. And then Beatrice saw her. It was Cynthia, riding like a queen on top of the pained painted elephant. No wonder the beast had cried out, thought Beatrice. The animal must have sensed the bad energy emanating from Cynthia. Cynthia's guards circled the poor painted creature, trying to keep it on course as they made their way through the bazaar, forcing vendors out of the way and knocking over rickety stalls en route.

"How could this be?" Christopher said to himself.

"I don't know, I really don't, but if you ask me, and I'm not one to know things, but if you ask me, this spells trouble," muttered Deepak, who was standing on his tiptoes to see above Sean's shoulders.

Beatrice knew Deepak was right, and she tried to hide her face as Cynthia passed them through the bazaar. But sure enough...

"So, we meet again, my little freeloaders!" Cynthia called from atop the poor animal. She ordered her guards to stop the elephant and force it to perform a low bow that would let her slip from its back. Beatrice wanted to run, but they were trapped.

"Must be your conscience catching up with you... you can't get away from me," Cynthia said with a smirk as she stood in front of them. Beatrice thought Cynthia looked even more unhappy now, as though the stress of her work was starting to catch up with her. She looked at her three friends, none of them knowing quite what to do, until one of them stepped forward.

"What is it exactly, if I may ask, though I know you haven't addressed me, so if I may be so bold as to ask, what is it you want us to do, given that it was quite logical that these three are not beholden to you in any way and that they acted with the most upright integrity, and..."

"Oh, god, not you again," said Cynthia, cutting Deepak off in mid-sentence. "What's in there for brains, you stringy dwarf? Can't you string a complete sentence together?"

Deepak stepped back, embarrassed, and one by one the friends turned and started to leave, disgusted again by the woman's cruelty.

"Come back here, just a minute," Cynthia called out from behind them in a voice that sounded almost kind. Beatrice didn't trust it. She knew there were many sides to the woman, and her face betrayed some sort of desperation. Her words seemed to contradict her face:

"Just to show you I'm as forgiving as the rest of them, why don't you come to a demonstration of new fishing techniques we're having later on the shore over there. It'll show you our company's intentions are good, we're doing wonders for increasing the prospects of these people." She turned to one of her guards then said, under her breath, "not to mention your share, I promise. The share prices will go through the roof when we get this technology back to the States..."

"These people..." Cynthia had said as though sucking on a lemon, full of sour distaste. And in her innuendoes to her guard there was something conniving, which made Beatrice's blood boil. Her thought-pictures jump-cut to Ms Buckley with her slow waddle walking through Stabroek Market, turning up her nose at the stall owners and fondling their produce with the air of none of it being good enough for her. Suddenly Beatrice is a double agent, dressed in black leather and a mask. She sneaks up behind Ms Buckley and lassoes her with a long rope, pulling her in and covering the screaming woman with a net. She lifts her up and, with the help of the stall owners who are cheering her on, carries the woman over to an empty lorry. The lorry driver tapes Ms Buckley's mouth shut and wraps her in airmail packaging. She becomes a tight package ready for shipping. They place her gently in the back of the lorry and instruct the driver to take her to the airport and get her on the first available flight out of the country. Beatrice brushes off her hands. Another job well done...

"Thank goodness she's gone," Sean said over her shoulder, jolting Beatrice out of her reverie. Cynthia and her gang had left the main bazaar and were headed to the shore.

"I'll attend the demonstration," Beatrice said quickly, feeling spurred on to find out what was really going on with Cynthia. "She's being nice to us for a reason. She wants us on her side, and I'm guessing that's because she's up to something dodgy. I have a gut feeling that it's something the people here don't know the full story of."

"Why do you say that?" Christopher asked.

"I agree," Sean jumped in. "She's acting like someone with something to hide. Did you see her with the elephant trainer? She handed him money every time he made the elephant bow to let her down or up, and I heard her say to her guard to take the elephant away and to make sure the man got another one for tomorrow."

"And what does that tell you?" asked Christopher, feeling one step behind Sean's reasoning.

"It tells me she's probably trading, maybe even poaching. I don't know... it's just a guess," Sean answered.

"I want to stop her," Beatrice said, calmly. "Or at least make sure we know what she's up to. Are you up for a fight, you lot?" she asked them all, looking into the eyes of each of them. They nodded in turn, looking proud of Beatrice.

Later that afternoon, the friends found themselves by the shore of the brackish backwater where hordes of villagers waited for Cynthia and her gang to make their appearance. When the huge entourage appeared, it was a spectacle of drums and whistles, with men and women riding the painted elephants. Some of the villagers had joined in, their faces decorated with red paint in intricate designs. Cynthia headed a long line of people who included her guards dressed in their uniforms, despite the stifling heat. Local fishermen lined up along the water's edge, watching suspiciously as Cynthia's group prepared mysterious-looking nets that seemed made of metal claws. One guard carried on his shoulders a metal and glass cage like a lobster trap, filled with water. As they reached the shore, music came from the back of one of the painted elephants. The crackled tones of a classical waltz creaked out from a loudspeaker strapped to the beast's rump, the music sounding absurdly out of place in this setting.

Finally, the ceremony began with Cynthia taking up a microphone. She spoke in English, and one of the guards translated to the public. "You are witnessing the dawn of a new era," she said proudly, with great pomp. She described her company. "You've heard of this new technology, I'm sure, but other companies are taking baby steps, while ours is making giant leaps in the forefront of massive changes that will do no less than change the nature of how and what you eat. We *are* the future. No longer will there be hunger, because we are changing nature. No longer will the women of this village have to stand up to their necks in the backwaters and pinch fish with their toes to fling them into terracotta pots floating on the surface. No longer will you have to mend the Chinese fishing nets that always tangle and tear. Now, there is a new way. And a new creature…" She raised her hand in the direction of the guard who held the metal trap. He took out of it one of two wriggling creatures. It was the size of a lobster but it had the shape and features of a shrimp.

"What you see before you, ladies and gentlemen, are two giant shrimp, a male and female, genetically modified to be bigger and guaranteed to feed a whole family with one of their tails. They are the only two of their kind, engineered specifically for this region," Cynthia announced.

"Oh, my goodness," said Deepak loudly. "It's hideous. I don't know much about fishing, no, not much, but if you ask me, and I know no one has asked me, but in my opinion you don't eat something out of the water that's that ugly…at least that's what my mother always said to me."

"I think I'm going to be sick," said Christopher as he turned his head away from the scene.

"This is too weird," Sean said simply.

"That man over there, that man, see…" Deepak said to Beatrice as he pointed to a local fisherman near the shore, "When Cynthia arrived on her elephant … I heard him speaking to the man beside him, and I think, I'm not entirely sure, because my understanding of the language in this area is not too good, I'm afraid … and, um, maybe I am being presumptuous to even suggest that I understood, but, er, really, this is a matter of great concern, because I think the man was saying that Cynthia's father had been under investigation by the local authorities for having been involved in a scandal with pollution some years back… seems his company was responsible for a terrible disaster … and that certainly doesn't seem like something you could overhear incorrectly, does it to you, Beatrice, does it?"

Beatrice noted the panicked look on her little friend's face and she touched his shoulder. "You're probably right, Deepak, but what can we do about it?"

She felt queasy, and as though there was more to this situation than any of them could really comprehend. She had never understood what all the fuss over genetic technology was about. When she thought of her own background and the long lineage of hybrid genes, she felt a bit of mix-up couldn't be all bad. But her father had complained about regulations and ethics and the fact that rice farmers in Berbice were having to buy seeds every year instead of just once, and that companies were making enormous profits while saying they were trying to help. And if it was true that Cynthia's father had been involved in a scandal here, could Cynthia be part of a new one?

"A shrimp and a lobster would never have naturally mated," Sean put in, as though having read Beatrice's thoughts again. Whatever the story behind Cynthia's motives or reasoning, Beatrice knew that she was a troubled person, and troubled people tend to spread their trouble. Cynthia treated people badly, and that was enough evidence for Beatrice. She wanted to stop her.

Deepak suddenly tapped Sean on the shoulder and whispered something to him.

"You two wait here, but be ready to run by the time we get back," Sean said. He pushed his way through the crowd with Deepak. Christopher and Beatrice looked at each other in panic. What were they up to? Beatrice thought she knew. She steadied herself, proud of her friends for springing into action.

Suddenly there was a skirmish at the shore. Sean had snatched the giant shrimp from the guard's hands and was making off with it towards Beatrice and Christopher. All at once the four of them were running through the bazaar, Sean holding the giant shrimp and Deepak trying to keep up, his short little legs doing their best. The guards chased them. Behind the guards Cynthia could be heard shrieking: "This is theft! I'll have you locked up for this! You good for nothing brats!"

When they reached the dock on the other side of the bazaar, Sean looked back and then held the shrimp up in the air. He shrugged, wondering what to do next. Beatrice grabbed the shelled beast and, with a toss, threw the giant shrimp into the water.

"Good thinking," Deepak said. "Without the other one, that one's not going to be able to mate and will just live and die alone, and that will be the end of it." He reached up on his toes to pat Beatrice on the shoulder. "Now we have to get the hell out of here."

Hesitating at the dock in front of a small boat, they wondered what to do.

"We're just borrowing it," said Sean as he leapt into the boat, started its motor, and urged his friends to join him.

The other three got in, and Sean steered the boat away from the dock. But they were pursued. The guards were in two speedboats, and Cynthia followed behind them in a high-speed racer. When they finally caught up to the small boat, the guards surrounded it, tied the boat to one of the speedboats and boarded.

They grabbed the four friends. Sean struggled and pushed one guard overboard, but the others were soon able to subdue him. They handcuffed each of them, forcing them into the speedboat. Off they sped to the far end of the backwater, towards a huge bamboo construction, which, Beatrice realised, was Cynthia's headquarters in Kerala.

"Consider this an arrest," Cynthia said as she got out of her boat, with sweat pouring down her face. She looked exhausted as she watched the four friends being taken away. "We won't bother with the authorities in this case, because they're... they're..." and her voice broke off, indicating a distinct distaste for even the idea of the authorities. "...They are incapable of justice... useless! But you'll have to answer for what you've done."

As they were being locked in separate bamboo rooms that
functioned as cells, the four friends were told that Cynthia
suspected them of being spies from another biotechnology
company that wanted to steal her ideas. Where had they hidden
the shrimp? She was determined to find out. When Beatrice
heard this, she realised Cynthia was desperate. The woman was
beginning to look more and more haggard, and Beatrice was
even more worried for their safety now. Before being locked
away separately, the four looked at each other and silently agreed
that they wouldn't tell Cynthia about what they had done with
the strange beast.

Later that afternoon, Beatrice was waiting in her hot cell, the
air thick with humidity and an odd smell. Her mind drifted off.
She was back in her spy movie with Ms Buckley in Guyana, but
now she was tied up in a cell, her black leather torn, her survival
instruments confiscated, unable to contact headquarters. Beside
her a large hourglass drizzled off the seconds as she planned an
escape. She heard cries from her companions, one after the
other, as the guards were interrogating them. She could barely
stand it. Her skin was tight and goosebumped as she imagined
what was being done to them. She imagined Ms Buckley's huge
teeth and her face that resembled the ugliest fish in any waters.
She shivered at the horror.

The rattling of chains at her cell door jolted Beatrice back into
reality. Into her bamboo cell came three of the guards. They kept
the door open but surrounded her so she could not escape. They
forced her to sit on the floor in the centre of the cell. A fourth
guard stood outside holding a long leash attached to something
Beatrice could not see. Then she heard scraping sounds, the
sound of claws on cement and of dragging hide. Then, right
before her, a crocodile appeared. Its jaws were muzzled by a
clamp that one of the guards now held ready to release. Beatrice
gasped, then remembered the ominous feeling at the sight of the
crocodile earlier that day. Cynthia appeared in the doorway. Her
face was flushed, her mouth contorted into a miserable snarl,
and her teeth were bared like a bottom-feeding fish.

"You know, I think all of this is actually your fault. You seem
like some sort of goody two-shoes. And you have the cute little
red shoes to prove it. Let me see those..." Cynthia went over and

held Beatrice's foot. "Mmm," she said, finding the shoes to her liking. She dropped Beatrice's foot and continued her tirade: "You probably think you're righteous and virtuous, don't you? Well, your little friends have told me all about it," she said, but Beatrice knew this wasn't true by the uncertain way her next words came out: "They say you know about the shrimp and that you're the one who planned it, from the beginning. Who are you working for?"

Beatrice was silent. Everything Cynthia was saying was absurd. What kind of bizarre universe had she stumbled into? A few months ago she was at home in Georgetown, bored by bad television, the silly boys at school, and the general lack of adventure in her life. All she had wanted to do was to get to Hollywood to go to acting school or to try for a part in a movie or commercial. But here she was on the edge of the subcontinent with this strange woman accusing her of spying, and a disgusting, scaly crocodile ready to pounce on command. She wanted to go home. She would help her friends to escape this evil woman and then she would go home. She fondled the locket around her neck. Realising her mistake, she dropped her hand quickly, but, too late, Cynthia had spotted it and reached out to grab it.

"Mmm, and what's this?" Cynthia opened the locket and saw the photograph of Beatrice and her smiling friends. "Oh, please, all you goody-two-shoes girls lined up together like a girl-scout troupe. My heart bleeds... and my stomach churns... how pathetic." She tugged at the locket, but it didn't come loose. She quickly reached her hands around behind Beatrice's neck and undid the clasp, and the locket and chain tumbled into her hand. Beatrice tried to grab the locket, but Cynthia pulled away.

"You are despicable!" Beatrice yelled.

"Oh, am I?" Cynthia answered, placing the locket in the pocket of her trousers. "Let's just say that's only the beginning of the repaying you'll have to do." She paused, looking at the crocodile, considering her next move. She took a stick from the guard holding the crocodile. "You think it's all a game, don't you? You've never had to deal with the responsibility!" Cynthia was pacing now, her face becoming flushed, her jaw tighter, trying to keep her voice calm as she continued.

"Just because we have to make some sacrifices along the way, doesn't mean we're not getting anywhere... they tried to convince my father of that, but they were wrong, I know they were... he couldn't have been wrong...but what they did to him..." She paused then turned to Beatrice. "Look at you... you've never had the kind of pressure I... oh, what's the use, you'll never have any idea..."

Cynthia was losing her composure, and with it her ability to express herself. Beatrice felt frightened. Cynthia moved towards the crocodile and made as if to remove its muzzle using the end of her stick. The beast shook its head from side to side, its huge jaws about a foot away from Beatrice's legs.

"I'm asking you one last time... where is the shrimp?" Cynthia said, her voice shaky and cracking. She held up the stick and was about to poke the crocodile into action.

"I don't know. I'm telling you the truth, I don't know."

"I don't believe you. I think you know exactly where it is." Cynthia poked the crocodile, and then placed the stick close to the strap around its jaws, where a flick of it would release the muzzle. Beatrice shrieked. The crocodile came closer.

As it dragged its scaly body along the dirt floor she thought of what it would feel like to die. She didn't want to die, at least not yet, and surely not like this. She thought about Felix and her Mom and Dad and about Stephanie and the people back home, how they wouldn't understand any of this. She thought of Sean and Christopher and Deepak who had obviously protected her by not telling Cynthia the truth.

"We let it go!" Beatrice said finally.

"You let it go! You idiots!" Cynthia stamped her foot. 'Do you know how much that thing cost to produce? That's one bill you're not going to get away with my dear. You'll have to be begging lots of money from Mommy and Daddy! Arrgghhh!" Then she stormed out of the cell.

The guards grabbed the crocodile's leash and dragged the creature out. They bolted the cell door from the outside.

Late into the night Beatrice was still awake. Her thoughts were not movie scenes but were plans for the future. She felt a sense of triumph over the horrible Cynthia and in a strange way even over Ms Buckley. She would not be dictated to by fear in the way she had been by Ms Buckley, who had worn down her self-confidence. She wanted to do something important, and she was now not quite ready to go home. She would go to Africa, as Linda and Eddie had advised her to. She knew that the secret Auntie Mavis promised was close now.

As she was pondering her career and where it might lead her, she heard the bolt of the door move. Light came in from the full moon.

"Come on, let's get out of here," Sean gasped as he gave her his hand and pulled her up.

"How did you get out?" she hissed as they met up with Deepak and Christopher.

"We'll tell you when we're clear of here. Let's go," whispered Sean. He patted Christopher proudly on the back. The four friends sped off through the bush and into the moonlit night.

Nairobi, Kenya

GREETINGS FROM NAIROBI

Dear Felix, It's safe to say that nothing
in your crazy imagination will come close to what has been
happening on this trip, so just go ahead and imagine. India was
an eye-opener, and Africa is proving more so. We flew here
without planning it much. Something about this trip was leading
me here anyway, but I didn't know it. We got on the first flight
we could all afford. Even Deepak is with us now. I will call you
and Mom and Dad in a few days. Tell them I'm fine and having
the kind of time I was meant to.

Love, Bea

December 7

Dear Diary

Crocodiles smell like sweaty shoes. I had one at my feet. I don't
know how to begin to write about it, but it was the first time I felt
that fear was something very real and physical, and not the ranting
of my brain and my inability to stand up for myself. I know now that I
won't be afraid to do so. I don't know how Sean survived his
confrontation with the beast, since he claims to be a coward at all
things, but he is not a coward. He is braver than just about anyone
I've ever met. He faces every challenge, and he writes about it. In
fact my companions are each very special. Even small, nervous
Deepak, who claims to have no wisdom, is the wisest boy I know. His
insight rises when he's not feeling nervous about being stupid, and
in those moments he is calm and like an old wise man. And
Christopher, beautiful Christopher is really a magical man. This is
how we escaped from Cynthia's prison:

Christopher had heard one of the guards crying late in the afternoon. In the man's conversation with his fellow guard, he said something in English about heartache and love. Christopher understood that the man's wife had left him and that he felt destroyed with jealousy and loss. The other guard wasn't able to offer any advice, and the broken-hearted guard felt even more despondent. He started to cry even harder. When he came to bring water into Christopher's cell, he was still crying.

"Sometimes crying is the only solution," Christopher said to him gently. The man looked up at him through flowing tears. At first the guard was suspicious of his prisoner's compassion, until Christopher reached into his bag and brought out some of his photographs. The photographs were of lovers, beautiful women, and even a few of new fathers and their babies. These made the man weep, but Christopher seemed to know what he was doing. He had one trick he'd never shown us. He told the man that he would take a picture of him looking brave and strong. He asked the man if he had a photo of his wife. When the guard produced one from his wallet, Christopher took it and tore it in two. The man gasped and grew angry, about to throw himself on our friend, when Christopher calmed him, telling him to trust him and wait. With his Polaroid camera Christopher took a picture of the man, then put it and the torn photograph into his circus hat. Shaking them around, he said the words, "true love never dies," over and over. Finally he tapped the hat and pulled out the Polaroid. This time when the guard looked at the photo he saw not only himself but also his lovely wife, smiling happily as she had in the photo before it had been torn. The man was so overwhelmed by this sight that he untied Christopher's ankles and let him go free. Christopher moved towards the door and looked again at the man, who was crouched over the photo, admiring it. The man looked up, nodded, then handed him his thick chain of keys, pointing with his chin to the outside. He was giving Christopher permission to escape. Christopher slipped out into the night, free and able to free the rest of us. We fled the compound as quickly as we could.

Taking a rickety coach to the airport in Kochi, we arrived relieved yet exhausted. And, once again, we ran into Linda, the beautiful flight attendant. By this point I was no longer questioning what seemed like impossible coincidences on this trip. Everything seemed to be happening as though scripted, and for a reason. Linda had been touring the south of India and had collected many spiritual objects and local potions. She had also been to see a healing man in the Lakshadweep islands. There, she told us, she had swum with dolphins and sea turtles, and she had learned how to cure colds. We were all in awe of her. She looked at us, screwed up a funny face and took a step back.

"Now, you lot. You look like you've been to hell in a handbag," she said, smiling.

"We keep running into someone who is making our lives miserable. A horrible woman who is up to no good, and I don't think anyone else - maybe not even her own company - knows the trouble she's causing, or how manipulative she is," said Sean, in anger. "We have to stop her, but I don't know how."

"Well, it takes all types to make up the world," Linda said peacefully. She took a compact mirror out of her bag and touched her nose with powder. She then took out an amulet and examined it. It was a small wooden carving of three turtles piled one on top of the other. "Like this?" she asked. We thought she had changed the subject, but she continued, "The key is to know who you are in the face of what you see. Trust your instincts. Don't forget you have everything you need, right inside you, you just have to listen to yourself... you'll get all the answers that way..."

She handed me the amulet and gestured that I should hand it around to the others. Her words and beauty had us under her spell, so we passed around the turtle statue, and I felt something strange in its magic.

"Where are you headed?" she asked as she put the triple-decker turtle back into her handbag.

"We don't know, really," I was finally able to mutter.

"I think it's time for Africa," she said matter-of-factly. And, of course, then there was no question in my mind that we'd go there.

And here we are.

In India the poverty seemed balanced out by the colour and splendour. But here, although there's light and colour, there is also bleakness. A visiting American doctor at the hotel we checked into this morning told us that two million people in Kenya have AIDS - 14 per cent of their population. And most women have about 8 children, and many have been born with the disease. What is happening to humans in the land of the first human? I can't understand any of this. I never knew such a horrible situation existed. There are also many conflicts among Africans, with tribes fighting disease as well as each other.

Christopher is upset by what we have heard. He keeps referring to the "first woman," the first human, as though this prehistoric figure is the woman of his dreams. He sees her as perfect, the ideal of love. Sean and Deepak also refer to the "first woman" regularly – her bravery for rising up on her two legs out of a life as a primate and into life as a human. The four of us have started to conjure her up in our imaginations, creating her as a magical figure who will show us the key to our lives.

We will spend a few more days in the city, but we are planning to go out on safari into the wilds of Kenya.

GREETINGS FROM ON SAFARI

Dear Stephanie, "Lions and Tigers..." Well, actually no tigers, but wildebeest, giraffe, elephants... and at night the sound of buzzing potential. The roar of lions or the cry of birds occasionally breaks the quiet buzz. We have a guide named Joash, who is 19, but he seems much older. He is a Gikuyu. Very beautiful. His face is strong and yet gentle. His eyes are dark, but they sparkle. And his muscles... Must be all the safaris he takes people on. I'm trying not to be shy around him, but it's difficult, as he too is shy. He doesn't talk much, except to Sean, whom he told that he would like to someday make a movie about his village. His mother has invited us to their village for a feast. Joash says it's a village that was once known for its lush green surroundings, but over the last few decades they've faced many droughts and hardships, and it's not what it once was. I am intrigued.

Love, Bea xx

The jeep turned down a dirt path and stopped just beyond the first row of thatched clay buildings on the outskirts of the village. Rectangular and circular homes surrounded a central meeting area with benches and a fire pit. A large well with a manual pump stood near the fire. Joash had an excited look on his face as he got out of the jeep. Anticipating seeing his family after months away in Nairobi, he walked quickly towards the centre of the village, passing people he greeted warmly. One of the older women took him in her arms, held his face and couldn't stop stroking it, as though she could barely recognise him.

Beatrice watched Joash as he headed towards a woman seated near the well with several children around her. The woman didn't look up, as though she couldn't bear the sight of Joash walking towards her. The children flocked around him, but the woman kept her eyes on her dishes at the well. When Joash reached the woman he said something. Only then did she look at him. Her face held a huge smile, and her eyes shone with tears and pride. Joash bent down to hug the woman. He lifted her up in his arms, which caused her to giggle and gave the children as much pleasure.

Joash introduced Beatrice and her friends to his mother, Wambui. She had astonishing eyes of bright green, which in this setting were strikingly unusual. Wambui's dark skin was smooth and youthful, but her shoulders were rounded and her hands were lined and callused. Joash explained that his mother had borne fourteen children; he was the youngest. Beatrice admired this woman whose eyes sparkled magically at everything she looked at. The woman reminded her of Auntie Mavis and Beatrice wanted to touch her, to feel the skin on her face and hands, but she resisted the temptation. Wambui took a special liking to Beatrice's red shoes. While Joash translated her words into English, Wambui told Beatrice that the shoes were like sandals in an old fable. Sandals that once signalled the village's prosperity. Beatrice blushed at the attention on her. She thought her red shoes seemed inappropriate in this Kenyan village, but she had become so used to wearing them she'd forgotten they might be conspicuous.

That evening around the open fire, after a filling supper of matoke and beef, Joash and his family told stories in their language, while Beatrice, Sean, Christopher and Deepak sat politely and happily soaking in the atmosphere of the warm night with the vast star-filled sky above. Beatrice couldn't keep her eyes off Joash and Wambui. Joash was so handsome, and Wambui so vividly brought to her mind images of Auntie Mavis.

When it was time to go to sleep, Joash approached Beatrice to ask her if she would like him to accompany her to her hut. Beatrice blushed with pleasure and said, "Of course." When they arrived at the small clay building he was hesitant to say goodnight. He lingered by the door and shuffled his feet nervously. He looked down at the ground, not catching her eye, and Beatrice was anxious for him to say something. Her heart was pounding and her skin felt tingly and alert. Finally, Joash took her hand, still without looking in her eyes. He held it for a few seconds and rubbed it unconsciously. She felt a rush of heat from her chest to her ears, and knew she was ready and willing, for the first time, to explore the things her girlfriends had been telling her about for years now. He looked up at her and their heads moved together slowly. They gazed into each other's eyes as though seeing deep into each other's soul. Beatrice's heart skipped beats. She had to gulp to keep breathing. When his face was just an inch from hers Joash paused and smiled. She smiled back at him.

"Good night," he said simply. "We have a long day on safari tomorrow and you must get a good night's sleep."

But Beatrice knew she'd never sleep now. She was steeped in the memory of his gaze and the potential of the near kiss. She tossed on her low bed all night and was surprised by how quickly the sun reappeared in the village.

December 10

Dear Diary
When Joash talks to me he looks me directly in the eyes and I start to burn up. Our talk is not just flirty; it's about real things, neither banal nor superficial. He tells me about the problems with his village

and in Kenya with the conflict between the two major tribes. He wants to leave Africa, but he has responsibilities to his family and doesn't feel he can be far from them. He wants to be an inventor and to study building and engineering. But since his father died when Joash was just 13, he and his siblings have had to provide for their mother and each other. Joash speaks of Kenya with sadness. He said that Africa could have been the most prosperous, most productive place on the planet if it hadn't been for the other countries that changed it, and for all the snags that come with kinship. Kinship, he said, meant that tribes kept to themselves and battled other tribes. Whoever you belonged to by blood you were bound to forever.

"But don't we all belong to each other?" he asked while looking up at the stars one evening. He looked back at me as we were approaching my hut. "You are lucky. You belong everywhere." Then he looked into my eyes and our faces came towards each other. We kissed. I had never been kissed like that before. I melted, and I wanted to keep dissolving, but Joash became nervous. He wanted to act as a gentleman. I giggled, a little embarrassed, and when he let go of me he bowed his head. But now I know what a real kiss is. Joash is shy about that part of things, unlike other boys I've kissed. It might be because we are around his mother and family, and he wants to be a gentlemanly son. Or perhaps it's something in his culture and traditions.

Around the open fire after supper, Joash's mother told us about a shaman of a nearby village who performs magic. Christopher's interest was sparked. The shaman has been working to increase the yield of the village's harvests, and to stop disease. But now he has to confront a representative of a very unusual corporation that is asking them to try experimental treatments and strange foods.

"Our food is very important to us. We know how to work this land. But this company wants us to accept their ideas." I was sure when I heard this that the man was referring to Cynthia. I knew by now that coincidence was a word I had to put out of my vocabulary, and I had to accept inevitability. Wambui wants us to go with her to visit the shaman so that he can tell us what he knows. If it is Cynthia they've been dealing with, we're all going to face big trouble.

Feathers, beads, and bones dangled in a necklace around the old man's neck. He described each of the pieces, Joash interpreting for the group. Each piece had a special significance, some magical power. The bones had come from animals. "Animals have spirits of their own," he added. "If you tamper with the spirit of a person or an animal, it may succumb to your power, but it will always find a way back to its essence."

Deepak listened intently. This talk of spirit power was not new to him, but it was from an intriguing source. He already believed in the power of the spirit, but had never considered it in animals.

"Lake Turkana has man-eating crocodiles," the shaman continued, "but perhaps that's a sign for men to stay out of the lake."

Deepak rubbed his elbow, and drifted off in thought, as though remembering the sight of the crocodile in Cynthia's compound. The old man continued to talk about the lake, Joash interpreting his every word. He told them about the Turkana, a tribe of pastoral nomads who herd cattle, sheep, donkeys, and camels, but who suffer from famine during times of terrible drought. Thirty years ago a Norwegian company came to their land to help them during a drought, and the company built a huge fish plant on the shores of Lake Turkana. The plant was set up in order to dry and process the lake's Nile perch, which could grow to four feet and longer and could feed the nomads, if only they would learn to eat fish and not meat. When Beatrice heard this, Cynthia's giant shrimp flashed into her mind, and she wondered where the creature was at this very moment.

"The fish plant failed, many millions of dollars later. Every thirty years or so part of Lake Turkana disappears, because the river Omo, feeding it, dries up from drought. How could the Norwegians not have understood that drought affects water? The Turkana have known this for a very long time. The two-storey frozen fish plant still stands but does not freeze fish. The Turkana call it 'the new mountain'," the shaman said. He asked Beatrice, Sean, Christopher and Deepak to help him get word out to the corporation people who had invaded their territory. He wanted to tell Cynthia that their own people knew for themselves what was best to grow and eat. He added: "and if you can stop them, you will be rewarded somewhere along the chain of being."

Sean took on the shaman's words as a mission. He, most of all, despised Cynthia and her manner. She frightened him but she also challenged him to greater courage. He wanted to go out on safari with Joash and to stop Cynthia from collecting animals for her experiments.

"We'll stop her," he said to the group.

Deepak quickly agreed to join him, followed by Christopher, and then a slightly more hesitant Beatrice, who wanted to make sure she would see as much of Joash as possible. When Joash volunteered to take them out on safari, she became enthusiastic about doing something positive for the shaman and his village. The group set out on safari early the next morning.

* * *

The sun turned the land gold as it crept up in the sky to the east, as the jeep made its way over the savannah. Beatrice could see an almost dry mist on the horizon, which she eventually realised was the rising heat of the coming day. Sun and heat were forces to be reckoned with here.

Sean sat with binoculars in his hands, raising them from time to time to catch sight of animals and to look out for Cynthia's convoy. Deepak fiddled with the loudspeaker and tape of lion calls that Joash always took out on safari. Christopher held up his camera and, with a special lens, was clicking photos of the wildlife and landscape. Soon a herd of elephants could be seen in the distance, near a watering hole. Joash drove on, not wanting to disturb them. A few minutes later a small herd of giraffe made its way gracefully westward, in search of foliage high enough for breakfast.

Suddenly they all saw what they had been looking for: a convoy of brand new jeeps speeding over the savannah in front of them. Joash sped up, but didn't get too close.

"Now what will we do?" Christopher asked.

Deepak, who had to be propped up on several cushions in the back seat in order to see clearly, turned quickly to him and said, "Nothing drastic, if you ask me. I mean, the way I see it is we should follow them and see what they're up to, catch them in the act. Poaching is illegal, and the least we can do is report them."

Beatrice noticed that his voice sounded sure and steady, with not as much stuttering and mumbling as usual. His hair was a thick, wild, matted mess and barely blew in the breeze that came at them in the open-top jeep.

They kept the convoy in sight as it headed quickly over the savannah, until it pulled up abruptly and parked near trees and shrubs that surrounded water. Joash brought his jeep to a stop. The hunters in Cynthia's convoy leapt out of the jeeps, carrying their guns. Beatrice grabbed Sean's binoculars and watched as Cynthia got out of her jeep, no gun in hand, but wielding a whip. Beatrice's blood started to boil. She remembered what the shaman had said about the soul of animals, and she imagined a beautiful giraffe tangled in this woman's net. She was fuelled with enough anger to stop Cynthia this time.

"Let's get closer," she said and turned to Joash with such an assured look that he immediately put the jeep in gear, and it crept slowly towards the convoy.

Suddenly there was a shot! Then shouting and running.

"Sounds like a gun has gone off by accident," said Joash. "Or someone has shot at an animal."

They watched as the hunters retreated towards their jeeps, their rifles still raised. Two of them put their guns down and lifted the carcass of a zebra out of a jeep. They dragged it towards the bushes and left it at the opening to the clearing.

"They want a lion, the carcass is bait," Joash added, as he drove the jeep even closer to the scene. He stopped, parked, and picked up his own rifle. He got out and ran towards the convoy, hiding behind one of the hunter's jeeps. He motioned to Beatrice to stay where she was, but her heart was racing. She wasn't going to let him be close to danger without being beside him. She leapt from the jeep, binoculars in hand, and sped towards the convoy, coming up breathlessly beside him. A few seconds later, Sean was at her side, then Christopher, then Deepak.

"Be careful not to make a sound. If they think we are a pride of lions they will shoot!" Deepak said calmly.

There was another shot, and then another. Suddenly they heard Cynthia's voice hollering:

"You idiots! How could you miss like that? What am I paying you for, anyway? Get it right next time."

"I have an idea. Wait here," Deepak whispered to the group. When he returned from their jeep with the loudspeaker and tape recorder he waved them on to follow him. They sneaked around the back of the convoy, making their way closer to the hunters poised with their weapons.

"If we pretend we're a pride of lions we might be able to distract them enough. Then they'll use up their shots. They'll have to recharge, and that will give us time to get in and reason with them," he said.

Reason with them? Beatrice thought. If only Cynthia was open to reason. She was just plain nasty. She seemed to be trying hard to make a point about her way of doing things, and maybe her father had something to do with it. If what Deepak had overheard was true, Cynthia's father had been in trouble for behaviour that was not unlike her own. But Beatrice knew there must be a loving side to the woman. After all, Cynthia had glowed with kindness when she felt attracted to Christopher. One thing was certain: Cynthia would not be happy to see Beatrice and her friends again. But the shaman had asked them to state his case and plead for her understanding.

Deepak led them, running in a line from jeep to jeep and around the back of the convoy, without being seen. They reached the trees where the hunters suspected the lions to be. Sean stopped suddenly and looked troubled. "If they think lions were here, doesn't that mean there's a likely chance they still are?" His voice quivered slightly.

Joash nodded his head. But he wanted to try Deepak's plan. They moved through the bushes. Deepak switched on the taped sound of lion grunts and cooing. They threw pebbles behind and beside the bushes to spur the hunters to shoot. The hunters took wild shots at the empty bushes.

When it seemed that many rounds of ammunition had been used up, Deepak had another idea. He whispered something to Joash, who smiled and gave the thumbs up sign.

Deepak played the tape louder this time and Joash joined in the lion calls, making deep-throated noises like a growl. Then the growl broke into words, and Joash was speaking in his language but sounding like a lion that had learned the human tongue. Beatrice could hear the hunters murmuring to themselves and talking quietly. They were listening to what Joash was saying, discussing it among themselves, and they sounded alarmed. Joash kept up his growling chatter and the hunters started to panic. Suddenly one of the hunters cried out something in their language and the others immediately dropped their rifles. They all retreated back to their jeeps.

"What the hell do you think you're doing, you idiots? Don't just leave those guns on the ground. Shoot, god damn it, shoot!" Cynthia shouted. The hunters were now in the jeeps, with their engines running, ready to pull out.

"Oh no you don't! I didn't pay you to be cowards and to chicken out on me just when we've cornered the very beasts we set out to find!" Cynthia cried. "You get back out here and pick up those guns or I'll shoot every last one of you!" She picked up a rifle and aimed it at one of the jeeps. She fired, but the shot went wild and soared over their heads.

That was enough to make three of the hunters speed off in a jeep. The others, with the exception of two of her most faithful guards, whom Beatrice recognised from India, soon followed and sped away while Cynthia continued to rant and rave:

"Get back here you idiots! You cowering, snivelling, good-for-nothing..." and these words prompted to Sean to leap out of the bushes to confront her.

"You were saying..." he said calmly, with his hands on his hips, facing her.

"Arrghhh! Not you! I should have known. How the hell did you find me this time, and what is it exactly that you have been sent to do? You are trying to ruin me, ruin me, ruin me," she said, stamping her feet and raising dirt around her. She flung down the net and whip in utter frustration.

The rest of the group appeared, one by one, from behind the bushes.

"Oh, god, the whole lot of them... and collected one more, have we little missy?" she continued, looking loathingly at Joash.

"We've come with a message, from the shaman in the Nyalgunga village. He warns you not to steal any of these animals, and not to use them for your experiments," Beatrice said calmly, terrified of the woman but feeling shored up by the words of the shaman.

"Oh, really? And what's he going to do about it?" Cynthia moaned. "Tell this shaman-guy that we're more magic than all the stupid bones and potions on the planet, and we're trying to make business here, see? And what's he doing about anything?"

Beatrice could see the fear rise in Cynthia's face. She decided to appeal to the woman's heart.

"They're trying to do things that are consistent with their beliefs. And besides, aren't there other things you could do to help get them better food?" Beatrice asked kindly.

"Like what, Little Miss Know-it-all?" Cynthia barked.

"I don't know, exactly, but..."

"Like distributing the food that already exists! Our waste!" interrupted Sean. His face was red with anger.

"Hells bells, here we go, bleed, bleed, bleed, my heart is bleeding you poor silly sap..." and Cynthia couldn't think of anything more to say. She caught sight of the two remaining faithful in her entourage, and a twinge of guilt rose in her face. She looked at Sean and then back at her guards. "Look, a girl's just got a job to do... I mean, really..." One of the guards moved towards her, but Beatrice wasn't sure if he was going to support or attack her. Cynthia's face went white. "I can't stop now, I'm nearly there... and I have to prove to them that he wasn't wrong... he couldn't have been wrong... he couldn't..." Cynthia's voice broke and she was close to tears. She stepped closer to the bushes, away from everyone else, wringing her hands as she looked down into them. Beatrice thought that maybe reason was working. She would tell her what else the shaman had said. Maybe that would help.

"And the shaman said that if you harm these animals their souls will wreak their revenge on you and you will suffer for it."

"Oh, now that does it!" Cynthia hollered as she turned towards Beatrice, no longer any sign of vulnerability in her face or voice. "I've had enough! Give me a huge break! Animals have no more soul than a rock, you silly little new age dippy doodle wanker."

"ROOOAAAAAR..." All eyes turned to the source of the terrifying sound that had shot out from the bushes at the very moment of Cynthia's last word. In a flash it was upon her: a lion almost the length of their jeep. Sean gasped and pulled Deepak out of the way. Joash threw his arms around Beatrice, and Christopher jumped back. They watched in horror as the lion pounced on Cynthia and went for her neck, tore at it, then shook the dying woman in its jaws until she was unconscious. It dragged her lifeless body back into the bushes and in another flash was gone.

Silence reigned over the entire scene for a few long seconds. Then one of the guards got out of the jeep and went towards the scene of the attack. He bent and picked something up from the ground that had fallen from Cynthia as she was dragged away. He came towards the five stunned friends. Sean was ready to defend them. He picked up one of the abandoned rifles and aimed it. The guard continued to approach.

"You've killed her," he said, softly.

"No, it wasn't us, really..." Beatrice said, afraid the guard was going to hurt them.

"Thank you, thank you," the guard said, and knelt on the ground before her, bowing his head. He held up something in his hand for Beatrice to take.

"I believe this is yours," he said quietly as he raised his head. Beatrice held out her hand and the man placed the locket in her palm. Beatrice opened it and saw, once again, the faces of her friends on the seawall in Georgetown.

The other guard jumped out of the jeep and came towards them. He took them by the hand, one after the other, shaking their hands, smiling and nodding.

"Thank you, thank you," he said to each of them.

"Oh, my goodness," said Beatrice. "I had no idea... it's not what we meant to do. We just meant to talk to her..." She felt awkward and ashamed.

"She got what was coming to her, Bea, and there's nothing else we can do about that. The shaman was right, don't you see?" Christopher said, coming up beside Beatrice and holding her shoulders.

The first guard started speaking to Joash. The others gathered round, and Joash translated for them.

"The company fired her a few months ago. They found out she had lied to them, and that her father's company had been sued for dumping waste, and the family forced to leave India. They didn't want to get into trouble. But she got even more determined then, and she blackmailed these two, telling them she'd get them sent to prison if they didn't help her," he said.

The guard shook Joash's hand and retreated to the jeep with his companion. The others walked slowly to their jeep and headed back to the village. The air was peaceful. Christopher put a CD into his player and Beatrice could hear the music and words from an Alanis Morissette song leaking from the headphones. "Thank you..." she sang, about India, terror, disillusionment and silence.

* * *

Wambui was stirring a large pot of stew on the grate over the fire. Beatrice, Sean, Christopher, Deepak, and Joash sat around the fire, watching it, watching her, mesmerised by her intensity and beauty.

"If you don't like yourself, then love seems like it takes effort. And that woman was like that," Joash said, translating what Wambui had just said. Wambui continued in a very soft voice, never looking up from her pot but addressing the four travellers.

"You all have exactly what you need, within you, but it's not until you love it that it makes its presence known. If you love something it appears, just as when you fear something it appears. What you fear is what you will get. That's what happened to Cynthia. For you, I hope you choose what you love as what you will get."

"Sean," Wambui looked up for a moment at him, then back at her pot of stew, "you have a knot of fear that makes you tense. If you invite tension it will visit you. You have done fantastic things, and yet you still feel that you are not brave. You are brave because you are writing your life. You look into yourself and you write about it. That's braver than being in a battle."

Wambui was silent for a minute or two. Sean looked down and began to draw pictures in the dirt with a twig.

Wambui looked up at Christopher. "Christopher, love is not something you find. Love is something you just let in, because it is everywhere. Don't be afraid to see that the love people give you is the love you are looking for. A heart is not measured by how much it loves but by how much it is loved by others."

Christopher looked over at Beatrice and his new friends, and he knew that what Wambui was saying was true. Tears started to trickle down his cheeks. Beatrice patted his hand, and he smiled up at her. They both looked back at Wambui.

"Deepak," she continued. "Wisdom is not in words. You are one of the wisest young men I have ever met. Do not be influenced by what others think, including your parents. Trust your own insights and then the words and the thoughts will be clear."

Wambui picked up a bowl beside the pot and began to dish the stew into the bowls. She was silent for a long time, and Beatrice became anxious, wondering what this beautiful woman had to say to her. Were there any kind words of insight that could help Beatrice? Why was Wambui taking so long to speak again? Had she forgotten about her, or was there really nothing more to say?

Very slowly Wambui rose up from her squat near the fire and walked towards Beatrice with a bowl of stew that she offered as she ran her hand along the side of Beatrice's face and brushed back her hair. The woman's eyes glowed with warmth. She spoke in her language and then paused for Joash to translate.

"And you, sweet Beatrice, you should know that you don't need to act like other people, you are a part of everyone. You are blessed with the blood of many tribes, and their ancestry is your ancestry. You must use this gift and tell people about it. You are welcome here, as a place to live," and at that moment she looked at her son, who lowered his eyes, blushing. "Someone like you can tell everyone else that where they were born doesn't matter as much as what they do with their lives. What's inside matters."

Beatrice felt choked up. She knew that what she had learned on this trip was that she was at home everywhere. Everywhere she had been people had recognised her in some way. Most people didn't see how much we are made from each other, and that we are the same deep down. Beatrice's looks proved that no one could ever be judged by what they seemed on the outside.

"But if you are not convinced yet of what I am telling you," Joash said, still translating for his mother, "then there is one last place you should go." Beatrice looked at her nervously. Why was she sending her away? She didn't want to travel any more. She was very happy here and would consider staying in this little village with Joash and his mother forever.

"The place you were born is made up of many conquered people. Slaves, poor people, people trying to escape their lot. Many slaves were gathered on the West Coast of Africa before they were taken to the Americas. It was a horrible place, a horrible time, and I think you should see it because it will help you to understand more. You have a story to tell."

Joash looked sadly at Beatrice. What his mother was suggesting would separate them. He took Beatrice's hand and rubbed it, a reassuring touch that said more than words.

Clearing up after supper, Sean, Christopher and Deepak approached Beatrice. Sean put his arm around her shoulders. He asked her to sit down with them.

"We think Wambui might have been telling you something important for you, since everything she said to us was absolutely right. Maybe you should go, Bea, but we don't want you to, not without us," Sean said.

"All three of us would be willing to go," said Deepak.

"Or maybe you'd like to ask Joash to go with you?" Christopher added.

Beatrice looked at them lovingly. They were true friends. She had never felt so warmly and fully loved, or maybe she'd never before allowed herself to feel so.

"Thank you. I think you're right, Sean, I have to go," she patted his hand. "I will go to Ghana, but by myself. And what will you do?"

"We'll stay here for a while, I think. I've spoken to the shaman and he says there is work we can do to help them with the food," Deepak answered.

"Then I'll come back, too, and see you, when I've seen what I have to see," concluded Beatrice.

She felt a rush of panic, wondering how she would travel on her own now, and she really didn't want to leave Joash. But she knew this was the toughest thing she had to face. Auntie Mavis would be proud of her if she did.

Christmas was approaching and she was homesick again. A part of her wanted to be in Guyana, with Felix and her parents, to be hearing carols, drinking punch de crème, preparing garlic pork with her mother. But she'd have to head back home soon enough, just after the New Year. This was her last opportunity to be sure about the secret Auntie Mavis had promised. She already had a strong sense of what it was. She packed her bags.

Accra, Ghana

December 25

Dear Diary

Merry Christmas. Christmas used to be my favourite time of year, but here in Africa, although celebrated, it doesn't seem important. The magic seems older, deeper, and I have continued to see things that seem like hallucinations but which I know are real. I'm sure I saw a man walking on the head and bones of another man, but when I looked again it was the ground he trod upon. I know by now you think I've gone crazy, but I have stopped resisting my own visions. At home magic seemed to be attached to Christmas, but here it seems almost ordinary.

I now regret that I left my red shoes with Wambui, for safe-keeping, and as a promise that I would return to get them after this part of my journey. I feel uneasy without them here, all by myself. There are so many interesting things to see. I have been here for over a week. Ghana is a beautiful country, and like Kenya there is a sense of underlying joy beneath what looks like the worst possible hardship. They love to play football here, and everywhere in the squares and cafes the old people, dressed in traditional Kente cloth, sit and play oware, a board game like backgammon.

By chance my coach stopped in a small village outside Accra called Dawu, and I decided to visit it. The tiny village has one paved street and one shop - a kiosk selling cigarettes, soap and bread. A portrait of Michael Jackson was painted on the front of the kiosk, with a slogan: "No Hurry in Life." It was a strange sight, and I'm still not sure why the portrait was there. The other structures in the village were made of reddish mud mixed with pebbles, and they had rusted tin roofs. The most alarming sights were the green trails of sewage leaking from the houses into the ditches that drained off into the surrounding forest. Between the houses the villagers had hung cocoa fruit to dry in the sun on elevated woven mats. The heat, the sewage and the coconut produced a sweet cocoa, fetid excrement stench that had me heading out of town very quickly.

In Accra I was shown how a drum is made, from the hollowing out of the wood to the stretching of the goatskin over the rim. All these things have been fascinating, but I don't feel the same about things here as I have on the other stops along this journey. Things have changed inside me.

I didn't want to leave my friends, especially Joash, but I know I had to come here, even if just for a short while. I now know that Wambui sent me here for one specific reason, and perhaps Auntie Mavis was speaking through her, because I feel like I have reached the end of my journey.

I am writing this while I sit on the steps of the Cape Coast Castle, the huge fortress built as a trading village in the sixteenth century. The images throughout the fort and those taking shape in my imagination are almost too horrible for me to describe. The fort is a huge city of dungeons and loading docks for the transportation of slaves. Painted images of the slaves being readied for trade and transportation to the Caribbean and America cover the walls. The information leaflets say that between twelve and twenty million Africans were transported across the Atlantic during the years of the trade. They were crammed into sailing ships, and for the five-week journey were fed poorly. Forced to relieve themselves in the same area where they slept, they were chained twenty-four hours a day and beaten regularly. Many boats didn't make it across the Atlantic at all. Thousands of slaves died at sea on the way to the Caribbean. The video set up for tourists showed some of the conditions as they might have been in 1664.

Horrible, horrible, horrible. How can people do that to each other? One of the slaves who survived the crossing was related to me somehow. I'm not sure how, and I will never know. But I know that he or she was treated brutally. There is so much brutality in the way we've all treated each other, African and European alike. Everywhere.

But the most surprising thing that has happened has been something else inside me.

Signs and pamphlets in the information office of the fort offer a warm familial welcome to Black Americans as well as people from the Caribbean. The signs welcome us HOME to Africa, reminding us that our origins are here. Something shifted in me when I saw these signs. I asked myself, as a person from the Caribbean, if this was my real home. Could it possibly be? Surely not any more than China or Scotland or India or the interior of Guyana. No, home was something more than this, something I shared with people on a very different level from "where are you from?" Everywhere I have visited on this trip has been like going to a part of myself. I'm sure that's what Auntie Mavis wanted me to know. And I think it is the same for everyone, not just me.

And you know what, diary? I now have no desire for Hollywood. I've had enough special effects fantasy on this trip to last a long time. I don't think even the movies could be as fantastical as all this! And I don't care about being famous or escaping my life.

But I do want to take all I've learned back to Guyana with me. This trip has been like a long story, and I want to tell it. And I want to tell other people's stories too, like a story about Ms Buckley at Bishop's or a story about Stephanie and Raj, or a story about Felix! I want to create something. So, in two days I will head back to Kenya to see my friends, and we will celebrate a New Year together. Then I must go back to my family. I'm ready.

No Place Like...

As the plane left Accra airport, Beatrice was lost in thought, retracing the stages of her journey and all the places she'd been. Her heart felt full, tapped into the excitement, fear and joy of the last six months. She took Stephanie's locket from the pocket of her skirt. Opening it, she looked at her own smiling face gazing out to sea. It was a face she didn't quite recognise.

The wild visions, the confrontations, and the final demise of Cynthia – these things had changed her. She still felt badly that Cynthia had been taken by the lion, and wondered if it had been too unfair a punishment for the woman's nasty ways. After all, perhaps she was under great pressure, and had been doing things to please her father and not herself. As Wambui said, Cynthia probably had trouble liking herself, let alone anyone else. But Beatrice was just beginning to understand life's complexities. Not everything made sense.

Linda agreed. Beatrice had run into her once again, as she was about to board her plane in Accra. Dressed in her airline uniform, Linda looked efficient and reliable. Beatrice was comforted by the sight of her across the terminal and ran over to her. When she told Linda what had happened to Cynthia, Linda shook her head and said matter-of-factly, "Some people bring the oddest things upon themselves, and we'll never know why. There's nothing you can do about that."

Meeting Linda in Accra, in yet another airport, didn't surprise Beatrice. Anything was possible. She posed the question to Linda anyway.

"In a world as big as this, how is it possible that I run into you so frequently, and in airports?"

"The universe isn't as haphazard as it might seem, I guess," answered Linda as she checked her reflection in a mirrored door. She brushed the hair on her forehead aside a little and then a smile appeared on her face. Without looking back at Beatrice she added, "And, besides, I am a flight attendant, you know," and she winked at her own reflection. Beatrice blushed.

"Here, try one of these. I concocted it myself," said Linda, taking a bright orange sweet from her handbag. Beatrice put the sweet on her tongue and was surprised by its tangy yet smooth taste. Delicious. Linda watched her intently as Beatrice sucked on the sweet and began to feel a bit dizzy. A feeling of falling, drifting on a cloud, came over her, and she struggled to hold on to consciousness. The odd feeling was like going back in time.

"What's happening?" she asked groggily.

"Nothing at all, dear, just a little something to help your memory..." Linda said and touched Beatrice's face. "Where are you going next?" she asked, as she turned around to pick up her bags.

"Back to Kenya, to see my friends..." Beatrice answered, feeling slightly more balanced. The mention of her friends made her confused. She wasn't sure who she was referring to, and everyone seemed mixed up in time. Did she mean Stephanie and her school friends?

"Well, I bet they're looking forward to it. I hope you and I will meet again someday," said Linda looking again at her reflection and adjusting her uniform.

"But I'm going back to Guyana, I don't see how that's possible..." said Beatrice, slightly more clear-headed.

"But you will always be able to do what you set your heart on. That's also a law of the universe. If you believe in something very, very strongly then it's bound to happen. And the things you do always lead to new things. Nothing is ever the same again."

That was for sure, thought Beatrice. She knew she couldn't go back to Guyana and be her old self – that self had gone forever.

"Hey, by the way, where are those cool red shoes you were wearing last time we met?" Linda asked her.

"Oh, I left them in Kenya, in trust really, so that I would go back to get them."

"They were impressive. I bet you could go just about anywhere in those."

Linda was right. Now Beatrice would take the shoes back to Guyana and show them to Stephanie. She'd describe for her friend and for her Mom, Dad and Felix, all the things that had happened to her. She had thought a lot about Felix in the last few weeks, knowing how he'd love a trip like this and that he'd learn to not be so mopey and so jealous of everything that everyone else had.

* * *

When Beatrice arrived back at Wambui's village, her friends greeted her with such a warm, enthusiastic welcome that she burst into tears. She went into her hut to put down her pack. There on her bed were her red shoes, waiting for her. She stared at them, feeling every step of her journey to this moment.

There was a gentle knock at her door. She opened it to see Joash waiting for her.

"It's time for supper," he said gently. She followed him out of the hut and he held her hand as he led her to the centre of the village. It would be their last supper together as a group. Before Beatrice left for Ghana, she and Joash had talked about her staying in the village, but she knew that it was way too early for her to get so serious with someone. She had things to do at home. That was part of Auntie Mavis's message.

Sean and Christopher were also preparing to leave the village. Sean would return to London to write the script about his days in prison. Christopher had decided to go with him and to start up his own troupe, a new kind of circus using the magic he'd learned about on this trip. And love, well, love would just have to be something that found him again. Deepak had found out from the shaman many ways to increase his strength and stature. He wanted to return to England and to study philosophy at a university, but first he would stay with Joash to learn how to lead a safari, how to recognise animal tracks, and to study the mysteries the shaman could introduce him to.

Beatrice, Sean, Christopher, Deepak, Joash and Wambui sat around their goodbye campfire in Wambui's village. A feeling of sadness seemed to rise out of the flames. Suddenly Wambui said something in her language, very loudly and vibrantly. Joash looked at her and smiled, while the others looked hopefully at him for a translation.

"The road you take to yourself has no beginning, no end, and no map has ever been made for it. But it is the only road to take."

The four friends looked at each other and smiled happily. Joash took Beatrice's hand and held it tightly. In that moment she had never been happier in her life.

* * *

The next day at the airport in Nairobi the atmosphere was sombre. Christopher's tears were flowing down his cheeks. Beatrice tried desperately not to lose her composure, but when she saw Christopher crying she couldn't stop herself and broke into a sob.

"Now, don't you start too," Sean said, bracing himself. "It's not the end. We'll see each other again."

"Of course we will," Deepak said with certainty. 'If not in London then in Guyana. We'll make it our mission to visit you there."

"Yes, that's what we'll do, for sure," Christopher said, sniffling.

Joash remained silent. He knew that it would be easier for the others to see Beatrice and the most difficult for him. He looked terribly sad. The others noticed it and gathered around. Sean and Christopher patted him on the shoulder. Beatrice stood staring at him, thinking that he was the most beautiful man on the planet. She hoped that one day she might find him again. The universe was not haphazard, Linda had said. That would bring them back in contact.

Over the loudspeaker a voice announced the last call for her flight to London, where she'd catch a connecting flight to Georgetown. She was going to be the first to leave. Christopher and Sean were booked on a flight later in the week. Deepak would accompany Joash on the drive back from the airport. Nothing would be the same again. Joash approached Beatrice and hugged her, then gave one last long and deep kiss.

"I will miss you, but you'll always be here," he said, pointing to his heart.

Beatrice didn't want to let go, but the final announcement for her flight came over the loudspeaker. She let go and moved to Deepak. Her mind became fuzzy again as it had in the airport with Linda after she'd taken the orange sweet. Time seemed scrambled. Deepak's face looked more and more like her father's. She kissed and hugged him with deep affection.

"You're going to be very admired for your wisdom..." she said, feeling sure of her words. Next she embraced Christopher who continued to weep. "You are truly lovely," she told him, and at that moment she had a flash of Felix's face as she wiped a falling tear from his cheek. When she approached Sean she could see his eyes shining with admiration for her, and hers shone back to him. She knew that if she hadn't met him in London and been intrigued by him, she would never have followed him and been exposed to the new world of filmmakers in Scotland. She might never have been on this crazy adventure. Her trip might have been completely different.

"You're wonderful," she whispered as she hugged him. She could almost smell the scent of her mother on him, so great was her longing to see her. Her tears flowed.

She put her head down and looked at her feet, at the red shoes that were getting a bit worn and shabby. She stepped back and looked up at her four friends. She blew them a huge kiss before heading past the barriers of the departure gate. She couldn't believe it. She was actually going back.

WWW.WORLDMAIL.COM

> Dear Mom and Dad

> No words can describe the adventure I've been on and the
> things I've seen, heard, and learned. I know you were
> worried about me for a while, and I haven't been the best at
> correspondence these last few months, but it hasn't been
> because I wasn't thinking about you. I've missed you terribly
> and can't wait to see you. I wonder if you'll see a difference
> in me (and not just that my hair is long and unruly and that
> I'm about a stone lighter than I was, just to warn you...). But
> I want you to know that this gift from Auntie Mavis was the
> best gift I could ever have received.
>

> I have plans for what I want to do when I return. I want to
> study. I want to learn the most I can and, in particular, I
> want to study art and filmmaking, and to one day make a film
> about Guyana that will tell my story. And not only that, I
> want to work with others to set up a place for other young
> people like me to meet and create stories, and to learn to use
> cameras and equipment to make movies. I want all of our
> stories to be told.

> Maybe one day I will go to Hollywood, but it won't be because
> I want to be a famous actress. It'll be because I will show
> people my films. Now I'm staying close to home, to you and to
> Felix. At least for the time being, anyway… I think Auntie
> Mavis would be happy, don't you?

> Love, Beatrice

GREETINGS FROM…!

Dear Felix, I'll be seeing you very soon now, and I can't wait to describe for you all the adventures, the tastes, smells, sounds, and sights. And next it's your turn. Save your money, work hard, get a scholarship, anything you can do, because you should know what exists beyond your horizons. The world is an amazing, exciting place. And Felix, there's no place like…